The Tilted Sombrero

OTHER BOOKS BY EVELYN SIBLEY LAMPMAN

Captain Apple's Ghost
City Under the Back Steps
Mrs. Updaisy
Navaho Sister
Princess of Fort Vancouver
Rock Hounds
Rusty's Space Ship
The Shy Stegosaurus of Cricket Creek
The Shy Stegosaurus of Indian Springs
Special Year
Temple of the Sun
Tree Wagon
Wheels West

The Tilted Sombrero

Evelyn Sibley Lampman

ILLUSTRATED BY RAY CRUZ

Doubleday & Company, Inc. Garden City, New York

1966

For Johnny McIsaac
with love from Gam

The Tilted Sombrero

1

"Just see that fine herd of bulls!" Nando's black eyes glistened with anticipation as he looked from his father, Don Anselmo, to his friend Cardito Garzas, who was riding a few paces behind them on a mule.

"A fine herd indeed," agreed Don Anselmo pleasantly. In response to a slight movement of the reins, the magnificent black horse he was riding came to an obedient halt as the man turned to inspect the dozen or so bulls who were grazing just ahead.

"But they seem to lack spirit," suggested Nando. "It is not good for a bull to grow as tame as a milk cow."

He turned to look over his shoulder at Cardito, whose brown face wrinkled into an excited grin. Cardito was able to guess the sudden idea which had appeared in Nando's mind on the morning's ride, perhaps because they had known each other all of their lives.

"They are eating. It occupies their whole attention," explained Don Anselmo, keeping his eyes turned on the herd. Under the tall sombrero with its rich decorations of silver, his thin, angular Spanish face seemed unmindful of the unspoken suggestion. Nando wished his father would turn so he could see his full face. Only Don Anselmo's eyes were a giveaway. They could fill with an anger so cold that it was like a wind off the perpetual snows of Popocatepetl, or they could lighten with warmth as tender as the new spears of maize which appeared after the first June rain. They could glow with an affection which the proud Castilian lips could not put into words and twinkle with amusement and teasing in a face which was otherwise without expression.

"But they have probably been eating since daybreak," insisted Nando. "It is now past midmorning. The *Inditos* have stopped long ago for breakfast and gone back to work. Only those fat, lazy bulls eat on and on. Their poor stomachs are never given a chance to rest themselves. And the more they eat, the more placid they grow. Isn't that right, Cardito?"

Cardito's grin widened but even on being called

upon he knew that it would never do to voice his opinion in the presence of the *patrón*.

Don Anselmo turned in the high, silver-studded Mexican saddle and regarded his son. Nando gave a yelp of delight, for under the bristling white eyebrows the dark eyes were twinkling.

"You suggest a *coleada*, my son? You feel that such a thing would be helpful to the physical well-being of the bulls yonder?"

"Yes, yes!" Nando turned back to the herd, his eyes making a selection. "I will take the second from the left, the large, black, ferocious bull. The one with the twisted horn."

"And the extremely long tail which will give you a good grip," nodded Don Anselmo slyly. He turned to smile kindly at the other boy sitting silently on his mule. "And you, Cardito? Which do you choose?"

Cardito gave a happy gasp. Although he was Nando's friend and most constant companion on the Hacienda del Fuentes, and the son of Don Anselmo's foreman, Porfirio Garzas, which gave him certain privileges over other peons, he still had to be invited to take part in the *coleada*, the twisting of the bull's tail, in company with the *patrón*.

"I will take that one," he cried eagerly, pointing with a stubby finger. "It is not so large as the one Nando chose, but see how he stops and paws the ground from time to time? He has fire, that one, I think."

"I think so, too," Don Anselmo smiled. "You have

both made wise choices. Now me, I shall take the large one on the far side. The one which stands a little aloof from all the others, as though he feels that he is too fine to mingle closely with the herd."

"Are you going to act the *coleador*, too, Father?" Nando stared at him in surprise.

"Why not? Have you no faith in your father?" The bushy brows lifted in pretended anger, but the eyes beneath continued to twinkle.

"It's just that I've never seen you. It was Ramón who taught me to twist the bull's tail. And sometimes I acted the *coleador* with Alejandro when none of his friends was here to amuse him."

"And who do you think taught Ramón and Alejandro?" demanded Don Anselmo severely. "I myself. It is because you are so much younger than your brothers that you have never seen me twist the bull's tail. Ramón was fourteen when you were born. Alejandro was thirteen, exactly your age now. It is true that I have not acted the *coleador* since then, but the old skill will return."

Nando tried unsuccessfully to shake off a little premonition of fear.

"Perhaps after all it would be better to leave the bulls undisturbed," he suggested uneasily. "It was just an idea. But it is beginning to grow warm and we've already ridden a long way from the house."

"It is already decided." Don Anselmo smiled at him affectionately. "I know what you are thinking, and I thank you for your concern. You believe that

I am an old man. You are afraid I will be injured, but you forget that I am in the saddle every day. El Rey obeys the slightest touch of my knees. With such a horse under him, any *coleador* would be safe. Besides, Fernando, you make me feel young."

He lowered his voice so that the words were for his youngest son alone, and Cardito sitting a little way removed on his mule could not overhear.

"When your mother died at your birth it was as if my own life was ended. I sent Ramón and Alejandro away to school, but I could not send you away, although the nurse was required to keep you in another part of the house. Then you grew older, and would not stay out of sight. I found that I was glad. Your brothers came home, and for a while we were a family again. Now they have gone again, but you stay with me, Nando. When I suggest that it is time for you to go away to school you say no; you prefer to study here with a tutor so that you can be with me. And I am weak enough to allow it. You have renewed my life, and instead of growing older each day I grow younger to meet your age." The soft voice deepened to a louder, gayer tone. "So I will try my hand at the *coleada* again, and if I fall from my horse then you both must pick me up."

Nando smiled with a certain embarrassment. He had never heard his father speak like this, so earnestly, so seriously, as though it was something he must explain. He had always known that Don Anselmo regarded him with a special affection. Of

course he was proud of Ramón, the eldest son, and
fond of him, too. Who wouldn't be? For Ramón was
handsome and brave, always laughing, yet filled with
understanding. He was a captain under General Calleja, and when he found time for a rare visit on the
hacienda the *Inditos* openly adored him, saying over
and over that he was a younger copy of the old don.

They were not so fond of Alejandro, and Nando
sometimes wondered if his father was either. Certainly Don Anselmo did not approve so whole-
heartedly of his second son and was always lectur-
ing him on his ways, which was probably why
Alejandro chose to live in Puebla de los Angeles.
There he found enjoyment in the company of other
young creoles like himself, who followed no profession but lived luxuriously on revenues provided by
their families.

Comparing himself with his handsome brothers,
Nando had decided that if it was true and he was
his father's favorite, it must be because he was the
only one left at home. Certainly it wasn't because
of his looks. Both Ramón and Alejandro were fair,
with delicate bones and slender frames. Nando, however, was short, even for thirteen, and stockily built.
His skin was darker than that of any other member
of the family, and he had wide cheekbones, black
eyes and straight black hair. If it hadn't been for
his clothes, trousers of finest leather, silk shirts and
gold embroidered jackets, he might have been mistaken for one of the peons. Alejandro had remarked

on this once and Don Anselmo had flown into such a rage that Alejandro, who had only just arrived for a visit, had mounted his horse and ridden back to Puebla.

"Well," said Don Anselmo a little sharply. "Will you ride first, or shall I?"

"With your permission, Father." Nando came to with a start. He must have been sitting there daydreaming. He narrowed his eyes as he inspected the unsuspecting bulls nibbling on the brown field. Perhaps he ought to disturb the herd, send them trotting off in every direction. But that wouldn't do any good, for Don Anselmo would simply take off after the animal he had already selected. Nando gritted his teeth, touched his spur to El Sable, and the horse started galloping toward the bulls.

The *coleada* of the bulls was a sport beloved by every male creole in Mexico. Compared with the Spanish bullfight, which resulted in the death of either bull or *matador*, the *coleada* was bloodless, but to the inept or inexperienced it could cause broken bones and painful injuries. A rider on horseback approached a herd of bulls, selected an animal, and, leaning from his saddle, grasped it by the tail. He then passed the tail under his own right leg and turned it under the high pummel of his saddle. A horse trained to the *coleada* would immediately wheel to a right angle, which caused the bull to tumble to the ground.

Sons of the Spaniards, creole hacienda owners and

rancheros who were taught to ride a horse almost as soon as they could walk, delighted in the sport. Even the *mestizos,* persons of mixed Indian and Spanish blood, who were restricted by law from riding a horse, attempted it on their mules. Only the Indians did not attempt the *coleada.* Perhaps it was because the lucky ones who owned burros had too high a regard for their beasts, or more probably because they were allowed no spare time from their sunup to sundown labors.

It was a dangerous pastime, for the horse's legs could easily become entangled with those of the falling bull. When that happened both horse and rider were subjected to a spine-jarring fall, and frequently to even more serious injuries.

The wind whistled past his ears as El Sable carried Nando straight to his bull. The legs of the black horse moved so fleetly that the victim had only a second to see they were coming. He lifted his head from the stubble, and the sun glistened on the cruel white horns. Nando glimpsed a reddish spark as the small eyes flashed in the startled dark head, then the boy leaned from his saddle and the extra long tail literally switched itself into his clutching hand. His fingers closed automatically around the round warm circumference, then it was under his leg and around the pummel all in one motion, as Ramón had taught him four years ago. As El Sable swung, the bull bellowed and there was a pull on Nando's arm as though his shoulder was being torn from its socket. He heard the sound of a thudding fall and felt El Sable's firm flesh tremble beneath him, but the horse held steady and Nando let go of the tail.

"*Olé! Olé!*" cried Don Anselmo and Cardito from a distance, and Nando replaced his sombrero, which had slipped from his head and hung from its strings down his back.

He tried to look becomingly modest as he turned and rode back to accept their congratulations, but he couldn't quell the triumphant sparkle in his eye. He had done well on the first try. Ramón would have been proud of his pupil. The next time he and his friend Captain Ignacio Allende visited the hacienda they would have much to say regarding Nando's progress as a *coleador*.

"Now you, Cardito," said Don Anselmo, when he had assured his son that it was a brilliant performance, equal to if not surpassing anything he himself had done in his own youth.

"Oh, after you, *patrón*," cried Cardito politely. "Please, Your Grace must ride first."

Don Anselmo seemed to hesitate a moment. Then he looked at the herd, which had gone back to grazing, undisturbed by the humiliation which had befallen one of their group.

"Very well," he agreed, and signaled El Rey to advance on the bulls.

Nando looked after him and his heart seemed to stop beating. Don Anselmo was still a superb horseman but he was, as he said himself, an old man.

Nando did not know his exact age, but his hair was white and there were lines in his face which grew deeper in the evening after he had spent a trying day.

The *coleada* of the bulls was difficult, and it had been thirteen years since Don Anselmo had tried his hand. Nando said a little prayer under his breath to the Virgin asking her to look after his father and not let him fall and break any bones. Old bones were very brittle and Don Anselmo would resent lying around doing nothing while they mended.

El Rey started slowly but all of a sudden he began to gallop toward the herd. The sun glittered on the silver trimmings of Don Anselmo's sombrero and saddle; it picked out the gold embroidery on his jacket, and then suddenly he disappeared. Intent on one especial animal he had ridden straight through the herd, and the bulls had opened ranks to let him pass. That was a trick of the most skillful *coleadores;* Ramón might have tried it, even Alejandro. But Nando never had. So far he had contented himself with one of the closer, more accessible bulls.

"I can't see," he cried in alarm, and touched a spur to El Sable's flank, causing him to start ahead.

Behind him Cardito kicked his mule with both hard bare feet and followed after.

The startled herd turned and trotted away, stirring dust from the stubbled ground where they had been a moment before. Nando's eyes tried to penetrate the saffron cloud, but not until he was much closer did he see a dark mass upon the ground, like a mound of rock, and as he rode through the dust he could tell that it was El Rey. In a second he was off his own horse, advancing through the stubble on foot.

The black horse lay where he had fallen, and although he tried to struggle to his feet one leg was broken so that his attempts were unsuccessful. At a little distance was a tall, crumpled figure in a gold-embroidered jacket. The silver-studded sombrero had fallen so that it covered the face, and the man was ominously still.

"Father!" Nando rushed forward and fell to his knees. He lifted the sombrero and stared into the silent brown face. Don Anselmo's eyes were closed, but his lips were smiling.

Nando put his head against the embroidered chest and listened anxiously. He could hear no heartbeat, but he was not experienced in these things at all.

"Cardito," he shouted to the frightened boy who was riding up on the mule. "Go to the hacienda. Get help. Tell Porfirio what's happened. They must send a carriage, perhaps a litter and a doctor. And hurry. Ride El Sable. He's faster than your mule."

"Me? Ride El Sable?" gasped Cardito. The suggestion seemed to be a greater shock than the fact that the *patrón* was injured. "Nando, it is not allowed!"

"I order you!" cried Nando fiercely. "Ride El Sable for help. As fast as he will go, all the way."

"Yes, *patrón*," said Cardito meekly. It was the tone in which he addressed Don Anselmo and Alejandro. He had never used it before with Nando.

He slid down from his mule and mounted El Sable. The next moment he was on his way back to the house, and Nando turned to his father. He was praying very hard.

2

"Fernando, you are making a great show of yourself," whispered Alejandro. "Come and sit beside me where you belong."

Nando shook away his brother's hand fiercely and continued to stand where he was. From the great hall he could see the long line of peons from the hacienda as they moved slowly across the cobblestoned square, through the carved front door, and past the bier which held the body of their late *patrón*, Don Anselmo. There were one hundred fifty *Indios* attached to the hacienda, with perhaps thirty *mestizos* employed in slightly higher capaci-

ties, so it was a very long line. When they entered
the hall they passed close enough to Nando so that
he could have reached out and touched them, but
although he knew each one by name no look of
recognition was exchanged on either side.

Alejandro sighed when he saw that he could not
move his younger brother and went back to sit in
one of the high-backed carved chairs against the
wall.

Since yesterday the house had smelled of incense
and candle wax from the tall white tapers at either
end of Don Anselmo's coffin, but now these odors
were beginning to be absorbed by a flower scent.
Each man, woman, and child who filed by to pay
his respects clutched a small nosegay of roses, lilies,
jasmine, poppies, or geraniums. These would be left
later when the *patrón* was laid to rest in the little
cemetery beside the family chapel.

It was three days since Don Anselmo's fatal accident. He had never regained consciousness, but
fortunately he had lingered so that there was time
to send a messenger for Alejandro in Puebla de los
Angeles, a half day's journey from the hacienda. It
had been impossible to reach Ramón. He was with
General Calleja, but outside of the authorities in
Mexico City, who knew the whereabouts of the
general? He might be in Monterrey or in Oaxaca, in
Veracruz or in Guadalajara. In warm climates burial
must take place the day after death. Ramón would
have to be notified later.

For almost all of the three days and nights Nando
had sat by the bedside of his unconscious father.
He blamed himself for the accident. Had he not had
a premonition, a warning that something would happen? Why hadn't he insisted on calling off the
coleada? Why had he permitted it to go on? There
were no answers, but he kept on asking the questions of himself again and again.

Then the rasping, irregular breathing stopped, and
Father Elizondo led Nando away. Alejandro came
with them, a strangely solemn Alejandro already
dressed in black as though he had known this awful
thing was inevitable. He spoke to Nando kindly, almost as though he might have been Ramón with his
deep understanding and sympathy, but Nando did
not hear the words, only the voice.

He did not hear anything that was said to him,
although almost everyone tried: Señor Buentello, his
tutor; Nena, who was once his nurse; Father Elizondo, and others. They even sent for Cardito, hoping that his friend could reach him when his elders
failed, but Cardito burst into immediate tears and
had to be hurried from the room.

Nando did not cry. He could not cry. It was as
though he were standing alone on a high hill and
everyone else was in the valley below and the wind
was sweeping their words away from him. Even now,
as he watched the peons file past him, he still experienced that feeling of numbness.

At last the procession ended. Father Elizondo rang

a small golden bell with his left hand and traced
a cross in the air with his right. The lid of the casket
was closed and the men who were to carry it took
their places at the sides.

When he saw this, Nando made a low moaning
sound. Then without a glance at anyone he dashed
out of the door, across the cobblestones of the courtyard, around the corner of the great white house,
straight to the corral where the de Fuentes' riding
horses were kept.

El Sable responded to the familiar whistle. He
came sidling up to the gate and when Nando flung
it open the horse stepped through and stood waiting.

The boy did not bother with a saddle. Long ago
he had learned to ride without one, and he leaped
onto the glistening black back, driving his knees
firmly into the horse's sleek sides. El Sable threw
back his head, whinnying with delight. This promised to be the kind of ride he enjoyed, a wild, free
canter with no certain destination, and with only the
warm breeze for company.

He was off, and Nando rode easily, holding on
only with his knees. El Sable was the master today,
free to go where he pleased so long as he took the
boy far away from this place of misery.

Gradually the wind blew the strain from Nando's
body. His tense muscles began to relax, his taut
brain reminded him that certain things had happened, things which he must accept, not try to shut
out of his mind. Don Anselmo was dead. Why it

had happened he would never know, but he, Fernando Genero Diego Rómolo de Fuentes, was still alive in this year of 1810, and he must readjust his life to the fact.

He had paid no attention to where El Sable was taking him, but now he realized that the horse had returned to the scene of the accident. There were no bulls on the stubble ground before him, but there was a freshly dug mound of earth which must be El Rey's grave.

Nando spoke a single word and El Sable halted, beginning immediately to nibble on the dry grass at his feet. The boy slid to the ground and walked over to the mound. Here lay El Rey, the splendid black horse of which his father had been so proud. And back at the hacienda, at this very minute, they were laying the horse's master to rest.

For the first time Nando's eyes filled with tears. He sat on the ground beside El Rey's grave and cried as though he would never stop. But after a while he sat up and dried his eyes, for his sharp ears, which Ramón teasingly claimed were keener than those of an *Indio*, had picked up an alien sound. It was a steady plop, plop, and it was growing louder.

A moment later a mule with a rider on his back emerged from behind a small cluster of low trees. Nando smiled. It was Cardito, his friend, who came searching for him. Good, faithful Cardito. Someday, when Nando was grown old and a *patrón* himself, he would find some special way to reward this loyalty.

Cardito brought his mule to a stop and hobbled him close by the grazing El Sable. Then, before he walked over to Nando, he paused to run his hands caressingly over the black sides of the horse.

"You found me, Cardito," said Nando. "Did you trail me? How did you know I would be here?"

"Where else would you go?" asked Cardito in surprise, settling himself on the ground. "I knew you would find tears in this place, so I did not hurry."

"But I didn't know I was coming here. El Sable brought me," gasped Nando.

"Ah, that horse!" marveled Cardito. "The minute I felt him beneath me I knew the horse was wise above all animals. It is a wondrous thing to be able to ride a horse."

"I suppose it is," agreed Nando slowly. He had ridden horses as long as he could remember, and took them more or less for granted. Impulsively he said, "When I am a man, Cardito, I will go to Mexico City and ask for the king's seal to entitle you to ride a horse whenever you please."

"You could not accomplish such a thing," Cardito told him sensibly. "You are a creole, because although you are of Spanish blood you were born in Mexico. Your father was likewise a creole, and also his father. To receive such an important thing as the king's seal one would have to be a *gachupín,* a Spaniard born in Spain."

"It is unfair," declared Nando hotly. "What you say may be true, but it is not fair. My many-times great-grandfather was one of the *Conquistadores*. He came here with Cortez. He helped conquer Montezuma, and destroyed all the pagan idols, and did away with human sacrifice, and brought Christianity to the *Inditos*. That was a great thing to do, Cardito. The king thought so, otherwise he would not have rewarded the *Conquistadores* with land, and *Inditos* to work on it."

"Ay," agreed Cardito politely.

"For three hundred years, almost, we have held the land that was given to my ancestor," continued Nando. "But because his children were born in Mexico, not in Spain, we are all creoles. And a creole is not allowed to hold an important office; he has no say in matters of government. He is only expected to pay his taxes, which grow higher every year. The king sends us, every few years, a new viceroy who was born in Spain. And all the men who hold important offices must likewise be born in Spain; the bishops in the church, the highest-ranking officers in the Army, the administrators—all Spanish born. They stick together, these *gachupines*. They say that they are the only ones entitled to make decisions, for they claim that the sun of Mexico addles the brain and we creoles are no longer sharp witted. That is why the *gachupín* cobbler, newly arrived in Mexico, has more influence with the viceroy than any creole in the province."

"Ay, so I have heard," murmured Cardito sympathetically.

"We creoles are aristocrats," declared Nando proudly, "because we have been careful always to marry women of our own station. The blood in our veins has never mingled with that of the *Inditos.*"

Cardito lowered his head without speaking, and in a moment the significance of his own words came to Nando. He reached over and pressed the boy's hand with his own.

"My poor Cardito. I did not mean—you must not think that I was criticizing you. One of your ancestors must have been a noble Spaniard. It is not your fault that he took to wife a native woman. Being a *mestizo* is a great cross to bear."

"It is not so bad." Cardito lifted his head, and the dark eyes in the brown face looked steadily into Nando's. "There are many of us *mestizos.* Thousands. More than you think. And every day our numbers increase. You are not aware of it here on the hacienda, but I speak with a true tongue. We are forbidden to live in the Indian villages because the *gachupines* fear we might stir up revolt. And we cannot live with the creoles, except as workmen, because you fear us, too. But still we exist. And someday it will be different."

"We're not afraid of you, Cardito," cried Nando. Again he pressed the brown hand with his own, and as he looked down he was struck by the similarity between them. The skin on both was of the same yellow-brown hue, all ten fingers were short and stubby, very unlike the long, slender fingers on the hands of Ramón and Alejandro. After a moment he continued. "Father Elizondo says we are all brothers, *gachupines*, creoles, *mestizos*, even the *Inditos*. Brothers in the sight of God."

"Yes, we are brothers. At least cousins." Cardito gave him a strange look and pulled his hand away. "Shall we go back now? I am afraid Don Alejandro is very angry with you for leaving the *patrón's* funeral."

"I know it was not right." Nando obediently got to his feet. "But I couldn't help myself. I feel better now."

Alejandro was indeed very upset with his younger brother. When Nando sought him out to make his apology, the young creole received him coldly. He was dressed in mourning black, as was Nando himself, but Alejandro's velvet jacket was embroidered with silver, and there were silver buttons decorating the knee openings of his breeches.

"You made quite a show of yourself, Fernando, in front of the *Inditos*. It was not seemly for a son of the house of de Fuentes to behave as you did. It showed a great lack of discipline and training."

"I am very sorry, Alejandro." He hung his head meekly, staring down at the black jet buttons on his heavy silk jacket.

"Well, what is done is done," decided Alejandro shortly. "Luckily no one was here to see but our own peons, and they won't talk. They never have. But it only goes to show that we must take steps to see that you do not disgrace our house again."

"What do you mean?" Nando lifted his head and looked at his elder brother a little fearfully.

Alejandro frowned and began pacing the long length of the tiled floor from the huge fireplace, large enough to hold a great length of pine brought from the mountain forests, back to the casement windows, which overlooked the huge square encircled by the various buildings of the hacienda.

"First, of course, you must go away to school," he declared forcefully. "You are far too old for a tutor, anyway. Also I think you should declare for a profession."

"Declare for a profession?" repeated Nando stupidly. "But by royal command there are only two professions open to a creole, the Army and the priesthood, and I'm too young for the Army."

"But not for the priesthood," Alejandro reminded him quickly. "It takes years of preparation to become a priest, but if you start at thirteen and bend all your efforts in that direction—"

"But I don't want to be a priest," cried Nando. "I want to stay here, on the hacienda."

"Impossible," Alejandro told him firmly. Then he added, as though speaking to himself, "Of course I realize that as the eldest son, Ramón will have the final say regarding the Hacienda del Fuentes, but Ramón is not here. He is a soldier, and enjoys galloping all over the country with his precious general. The hacienda and its maintenance must fall on my shoulders, and I have certain plans for it. I shall continue to live in Puebla, of course, but from time to time I shall bring parties here for a few weeks. Many of my friends live in Puebla and entertain at their nearby haciendas."

"But I could stay here and keep an eye on it while you are in Puebla," volunteered Nando eagerly. "I know all about overseeing. I rode every day with Father. And the peons like me."

"I don't wonder." Alejandro turned and looked at him critically.

Under his frankly disapproving gaze, Nando felt very small. He's thinking again that I look like an Indian, he told himself miserably. Then he remembered that Alejandro was his blood brother, that they were both creoles and aristocrats, and he returned the look proudly.

"The priesthood is the only answer," said Alejandro, and this time his voice was a little sympathetic. "It isn't fair. It's unfortunate, and I don't see how it could have happened after all these years. But there it is. You have only to look in the mirror to see it for yourself."

"See what? What are you talking about?" cried Nando in alarm. He wondered frantically if he were coming down with some dreadful spotted disease, the effects of which were beginning to pop out.

"You don't know, do you?" asked Alejandro

kindly. He motioned for Nando to sit down in one of the heavy carved chairs upholstered in soft tanned leather. When the boy had done so, he took the one opposite.

"It is not a pretty story, Fernando, and it is one which we have tried very hard to keep hushed up," he began apologetically. "It concerns our great-grandfather, Don Genaro de Fuentes. He was married to a lady from Barcelona. Doña Rosaura Maldonado—"

"I know," nodded Nando. "Our great-grandmother. I have seen the little painting of her face. She was very beautiful."

Alejandro looked at him strangely.

"She died young. For two years only was the Doña Rosaura mistress of this hacienda, and in that time she did not give our great-grandfather, Don Genaro, a child."

"Then how—"

"Soon after her death, Don Genaro took a native woman to wife." Alejandro held up his hand for silence. He spat out the words as though they were very unpleasant to him. "Perhaps he had a premonition that he himself would die shortly. Perhaps he thought—I do not know what he thought, only what he did. He had a son by this woman, one child only, who was our grandfather."

"Then we are not creole," cried Nando in amazement. "We are *mestizo!*"

"We are creole! Creole, I tell you!" Alejandro

stood up and shouted his declaration. His thin, finely boned face grew very sharp, and staring up at him Nando could see no hint of that Indian great-grand-mother. Only she was there. Her blood, which flowed in Alejandro's veins, and Ramón's and his own had made itself evident in him.

Alejandro regained his composure and sat down again in the carved chair.

"Only our people on the hacienda knew of this thing," he continued in his normal tone. "And they, of course, dared not speak. Don Genaro kept the child hidden until it was old enough so that it was impossible to guess the exact age, then he told people that it was Doña Rosaura's and that she had died in childbirth. Luckily our grandfather favored his father. He showed none of the Indian blood, nor did our father."

"And neither do you or Ramón," said Nando slowly. "But I do. I am the *mestizo*."

"No, no." Alejandro leaned over and the long, slender Castilian hand patted Nando's knee. "You, too, are a creole. You must never think otherwise. You must never say otherwise. Promise me that you will not. Swear by our mother's sacred memory that you will never call yourself *mestizo* again."

"I swear," whispered Nando feebly. His head was buzzing with this shocking revelation, and the only comforting thought was that the disgrace had been shared by Don Anselmo and was being shared now by Alejandro and Ramón.

"There are many creole families, aristocratic families like ours, who hide similar skeletons in their closets," said Alejandro. "The old families particularly. In three hundred years it could not be otherwise. I have heard that sometimes there appears a child like you who shows only the Indian strain. I understand it is the accepted thing for him to enter the church, either as a nun or a priest."

"Oh!"

So that was why Alejandro was urging the priesthood on him. It was an attempt to bury him from public life. If Nando was far away, serving as *cura* in some distant village, his family would not have to make excuses.

Alejandro's story had made so many things clear to him, things he could not understand before. It explained Cardito's strange look this morning when he said if they were not brothers at least they were cousins. It explained why Alejandro had never brought his fastidious creole friends to visit on the hacienda. He did not want them to see Nando, who betrayed the Indian blood. Perhaps it explained the slight coolness which had always existed between himself and Alejandro, a coolness which he had never felt with Ramón.

"Does Ramón know?" he asked suddenly. A picture of his eldest brother came to his mind, handsome, dashing, affectionate. Ramón brought friends to the hacienda. In recent years, his army years, it had always been Don Ignacio Allende, a young

captain who served with Ramón under General Calleja. Don Ignacio had eyes. Perhaps he had wondered about the youngest son of the family. But he
was a gentleman, as Ramón was a gentleman. Certain things are ignored between gentlemen. They
are never mentioned aloud.

"Of course Ramón knows." Alejandro seemed surprised. "Our father told us both on our eighteenth
birthdays, as he would have told you on yours. Or
perhaps," he decided thoughtfully, looking at Nando's blunt features, "he might not have told you.
Perhaps he would have kept the secret. But you
are one of the family. I think it is fair that you
should know."

"It is fair," agreed Nando soberly.

"Now about the plans for your future." Alejandro
spoke cheerfully, as though a great load had been
lifted from his shoulders. "Under the circumstances,
don't you feel it is wise for you to declare as a
priest?"

"Yes. It is wise," admitted Nando. "You are my
elder brother. I will do as you wish."

"Good. At the end of the week we will go to
Puebla de los Angeles. You can take a *diligencia*
there for Mexico City, where you can enroll as a
student. Our father's old friend Don Manuel Hidalgo
will help you. He is a *licenciado* there and also a
member of the *Inquisición*. I will write a letter for
you to carry."

The predominant blood of the conquerors won

over the smaller Indian strain and Nando lifted his head proudly.

"I will not go by *diligencia*," he declared haughtily. "I will ride El Sable to Mexico City."

Alejandro looked at him in surprise.

"Of course." His tone was of mild amusement. "It shall be as you wish."

3

Nando handed El Sable's reins to the Indian who had taken charge of Alejandro's horse and followed his brother up the stone steps which led to the Cathedral of the Immaculate Conception.

It was the first time in his life that he had ever been in Puebla. Don Anselmo had often remarked that one day they would visit this great city founded by the Spaniards in 1531, but somehow they had never managed to get here. In the face of his new knowledge, Nando wondered if his father, too, had been ashamed of the Indian features of his son and that was why they had never come.

Alejandro was ashamed of them. Nando was positive of that. They had been here three days waiting for a *diligencia* to Mexico City, and in all that time Alejandro had not invited one friend to his house, nor had he taken Nando out in public.

Today, however, was different. Alejandro had ordered a mass in the great cathedral for the soul of his father, Don Anselmo, and the bishop had selected today for the service. Naturally the younger son must be present. If it could only have been delayed twenty-four hours, thought Nando resentfully, he would have been on his way, for the *diligencia* to Mexico City left early tomorrow morning.

Since Nando had never before left the hacienda, he had not understood about the *diligencia*. He thought it was some sort of vehicle. It wasn't at all. He was to ride El Sable, but he must go in a great company of coaches and horsemen traveling together for mutual protection against robbers. That was the meaning of the word *diligencia*, and it was why Alejandro had been so amused when Nando insisted on riding horseback.

Now as he followed Alejandro's black velvet back up the stairs, Nando stared at the majestic stone cathedral pushing upward against the blue sky. It was built on a terrace which made the two great bell towers look even taller than they were. Nando remembered the story people still told about its erection. They said that during the night, after the laborers had laid away their tools, angels continued on with the work and that was why such a magnificent edifice went up so rapidly.

At the great carved doorway, Alejandro glanced over his shoulder to make sure Nando was coming. But Nando had no intention of running away now as he had on the familiar hacienda. He was overwhelmed by the magnitude of the cathedral, and he stayed close behind his brother's stiff back lest he become lost. When Alejandro dipped his fingers in the holy water, Nando did the same, marveling at the marble and gold basin. Then he noticed that the very floor on which they walked was polished marble.

There were many broad aisles, divided by massive stone columns, but Alejandro knew which one to choose. They passed inlaid stalls, exquisitely carved, and there was not one but several altars, each with its own magnificent statuary. Everything was gold-encrusted, and the air was so heavy with incense that Nando had difficulty suppressing a sneeze.

At last Alejandro stopped and, dropping to his knees, he motioned to Nando to do likewise. It was the time for a prayer, a private prayer for the soul of Don Anselmo, but Nando didn't know what to ask. He couldn't help feeling that his father, like himself, would have been overwhelmed by this splendor, for Don Anselmo was a simple man and the little chapel at the hacienda was simple.

Nando did not hear much of the service, but he did not think his father would have minded. Be-

sides, it was in Latin, which he could not understand. Instead of listening he studied the magnificent
paintings in their huge golden frames which hung
on the walls and inspected the rich embroidered
vestments of the priests, wondering if he himself
would someday wear any so fine, or if he must be
content with patched black, like the *curas* in the
small villages nearer home. Perhaps, if he applied
himself, he could become a *licenciado*, a lawyer, as
was his father's friend Manuel Hidalgo. The ap-
pointments of *licenciados* were made through the
church, and so open to creoles. They were usually
given to certain advanced theological students who
might be useful in the works of the *Inquisición*.

There were a great many people attending the
mass. Probably it was because Alejandro had sent
out cards inviting them. They must be his friends,
and as Nando began studying them he was suddenly
conscious that several were inspecting him in turn.
He could read curiosity on their faces, and he felt
his cheeks begin to burn as he knew what they
must be thinking.

Poor Alejandro! He had been so proud of his
pure Castilian blood. He had never brought anyone
home, but now, through no fault of his own, the
dark smear was out in public where it could not be
missed.

Nando edged as far away from his brother as
possible. Perhaps they would think him a very dis-

tant relation. He didn't want Alejandro to suffer on his account.

At last it was over. The people rose to their feet. They began to file out, and Alejandro turned to Nando with a smile.

"I am sure the mass did much good. It was very expensive. Our father is a step closer to heaven now."

"Will your friends be waiting outside to talk with you?" demanded Nando harshly.

"Some of them, yes." Alejandro's eyebrows lifted with surprise. "After this mass they will feel free to resume our friendships as before. Good manners would restrain them from calling on us until now."

"Then I will go back to your house. I do not wish to talk with anyone."

"You were very close to our father, closer than Ramón or I. It is natural that you should be moved by his fine mass," decided Alejandro. "But you cannot ride to my house alone. You do not know the way. You must wait for me."

He turned to leave the cathedral and Nando followed miserably. He had never been fond of Alejandro, but in the last week his brother had done his best to be kind. True, he was advising that Nando hide himself in a monastery, but if that was the accepted thing in cases like his own, it was a natural suggestion. He lifted his head, swearing to himself that despite his Indian features he would conduct himself with the gracious pride of any creole.

Once he was outside, however, his resolve faded rapidly. Alejandro was busy greeting friends, handsome young creoles like himself, suitably dressed in mourning black, but resplendent with flashing diamonds, pearls, and rubies. He seemed to have forgotten Nando standing alone in the great carved doorway, and Nando did not wish to intrude. He walked slowly down the wide, flat steps toward the wrought iron fence which encircled the cathedral square.

As he reached the gates he looked back. Alejandro had left the young cavaliers and was now speaking with a family group. There were two dignified older men and two black-veiled women of the same age, quite a beautiful younger lady in a black lace mantilla over whose hand Alejandro was bowing, and a girl about a year younger than Nando. Like her elders, the girl wore mourning for the recent mass, but she had pushed back her veil so that she could see more clearly. The face which looked out of the black folds was round, and so were the gray eyes which were staring straight at Nando.

When she saw him looking at her she smiled. It was a wide, friendly smile, but to Nando it was also a knowing smile, as though she might be laughing at him. It was the last straw. He flounced out of the gate and hurried toward the Indian who was patiently holding El Sable.

"The road to Mexico City?" demanded Nando angrily. "Show it to me."

The Indian made a surprised, unintelligible reply, but one finger pointed the direction. Nando was on the back of El Sable in the instant. He would not wait for the *diligencia* after all. He would take himself away from Puebla and off Alejandro's hands now.

He was well out of town before he began to realize that he might have been a little hasty. Here he was traveling alone, with only the clothes on his back and a pitifully few *reales* in his pocket. The road was strange, and Mexico City, when he reached there, would be even bigger and more frightening than Puebla. It was a hundred miles away. It would take at least two days to reach there, providing he was lucky. Where would he stay? What would he eat? And how would he ever find the *Licenciado* Hidalgo in such a vast place?

The sensible thing to do was to turn El Sable and return to Puebla. He could ask someone to show him Alejandro's house, and when he arrived confess that he had made another mistake. But pride wouldn't let him do this. He had taken matters into his own hands, now he must go on.

At first the road leading from Puebla was level. It led through cultivated fields, doubtless belonging to some hacienda, or to one of the *rancheros* who owned smaller estates. The Hacienda del Fuentes had grown mostly corn, but here Nando saw fields given over to wheat, beans, *garbanzos*, barley, and, of course, *maguey*. There were orchards of fruit trees, too, and he was reminded of the old Spanish proverb, "If you live in the Indies, let it be within sight of the volcanoes." People said there was something about volcanic peaks which made the soil fertile, and certainly the crops of this district proved it.

Nando had glimpsed the distant snowy mountains when he and Alejandro had first ridden into Puebla, and this road seemed to lead directly toward them. With every step El Sable brought them closer. Popocatepetl, the smoking mountain, Ixtaccihuatl, the sleeping woman, and Malinche, named after the Mexican wife of Cortez. Cortez had a native wife, Nando thought suddenly, and he had heard they had a son, a son who was accorded a title by the King of Spain. No one called the son of Cortez a *mestizo*, but that's what he was.

He passed through several small villages, stopping once for El Sable to drink from the town fountain and to rest awhile. He might have stayed longer beneath the shade trees of the square but he realized that people were looking at him strangely. Well, why not? He was not known here, and his Indian face contrasted with the silk clothes of a gentleman must have looked strange to them. When he saw that they were looking from him to El Sable, he climbed hastily into the saddle. Someone might ask to see his king's seal which would permit him to ride a horse.

By late afternoon Nando had left the cultivated fields behind. The road was beginning to climb, and ahead were the forests. This was the dangerous part, he remembered with a little panic, the reason why travelers journeyed together. The forests were filled with robbers.

He signaled El Sable to a willing halt. Perhaps it would be wise to ride back to the last village where he could buy food. He had not eaten since early morning and he was very hungry. As he sat there, deciding what he should do, he found himself surrounded by a band of mounted men. They had ridden out from the protection of the trees, and they had come so silently that they were upon him before he knew it.

They were a dozen or more in number, and most of their mounts were mules or burros. One or two had horses, rather inferior horses Nando decided, contrasting them automatically with those in his family's stables, but the horseback riders were not creole gentlemen. They were *mestizos*, and they flourished ponderous black firearms. The mule and burro riders carried only whips and knives, but for these Nando had an even healthier respect than for the guns.

"What have we here?" demanded one of the horseback riders who seemed to be the leader. His badly soiled and torn clothing was of the fine quality affected by the upper classes. But it was his sombrero which made Nando's eyes widen with alarm.

It was worn low on his forehead, so that it concealed the upper part of his face. Only that portion from the nose down was visible. Without question, it marked the man as a bandit.

Nando had never seen one before, but he had heard of them. Porfirio, foreman on the hacienda, had told him and Cardito all about them. They always wore their sombreros low, shading their eyes.

"That is because they are wicked," Porfirio had explained solemnly. "They do not want strangers to view the evil in their eyes. An honest man wears his sombrero tilted on the back of his head. Then all the world can see that he is what he claims to be."

The bandit leaned from his saddle, his dirty hand touching El Sable's coat.

"A fine horse," he said approvingly.

"How dare you?" demanded Nando. He pulled El Sable back, away from the greedy touch. "Tell your men to move away and let me through."

"Why, he's only a boy. A lad," laughed the man in surprise. He leaned closer to peer into Nando's face. "And an *Indito!* Or a *mestizo*, at least, parading in the clothes of a gentleman. And riding on a stolen horse besides."

"He's not stolen. He's mine. And I'm not a *mestizo*. I am a creole. I am Fernando Genero Diego Rómolo de Fuentes."

"And I am the viceroy of Mexico, at your service, señor," announced the bandit solemnly, causing loud shrieks of laughter from his men.

"If he is a creole, we could get a ransom from his family, José," called one of the crowd.

"A creole? This one? Have you looked at his face? No, this is some young thief. And as good subjects of his majesty it is our duty to relieve him of his stolen goods. Get down on the ground, boy."

"I won't," declared Nando angrily.

There was a whizzing sound as one of the long whips curled in the air. Before Nando could protect himself it had wound around his shoulders, and the next moment he was in the dust of the road.

"A beautiful animal," observed the bandit leader, inspecting El Sable from every side. "I will ride it myself. Nacho, you may have my old horse. Give your mule to someone who has only a burro."

"May I have his clothes, José?" pleaded a shrill voice. "I think this boy's garments would fit me exactly."

José was dismounting from his horse. Now he turned and smiled at the speaker, a boy about Nando's age.

"Of a certainty you may have his clothes, Pedro. Take them off, boy," he ordered Nando.

"I won't!"

"Would you like the whip again?" asked José pleasantly. He began lengthening El Sable's stirrups to fit his own longer legs.

"No," said Nando sullenly. If he didn't remove his clothes himself, they would take them from him. He began unbuttoning his jacket.

"And to show you we are not bad fellows, you shall have Pedro's clothes," decided José grandly.

Nando looked at the dirty white cotton pants, the loose white jacket with one sleeve nearly torn from the shoulder, and the frayed straw sombrero. Even the lowliest *Indio* on the Hacienda del Fuentes had better clothes than those.

"Let him have my burro, too," cried Pedro eagerly. "I will take Nacho's mule."

"Ay, a burro is another thing, *chico*," laughed the leader, leaping to his seat in El Sable's silver-studded saddle. "There are many uses for a burro."

"Of course you will leave me on foot," declared Nando haughtily. "That is the way of bandits, I am told. They take all. All that there is to take."

"Not so, boy," contradicted the leader indignantly. "Of bandits, possibly. Of traders, no. And we are traders. You have helped us by giving us your horse and your clothes. We have given you clothes in return, so it is merely a trade. Where are you going?"

"To Mexico City."

"A long way, surely. A burro would be of help. We will trade you one. One burro for one horse. Now, you see we are not bandits at all!"

Nando stood there helplessly watching Pedro scramble into his silk clothes and the bandit leader parade back and forth on El Sable's back. The dirty white garments of the robber boy lay in a pile at his feet. He hated to touch them, much less put them on.

At last Pedro announced that he was ready. He gave a few yelps of protest when he found he was not to have the mule after all. One of the older men had already claimed it.

With much shouting and laughter the band rode away, back into the shadows of the forest, and Nando was left alone. One burro, without a blanket, remained behind. Sadly the boy leaned over and began putting on the dirty white clothes at his feet.

4

At first Nando had considered leaving the burro behind. It would be a scornful gesture, worthy of an aristocratic creole, to refuse what amounted to an outright gift from the robber chief. Common sense told him that he could not afford to do so. The purse containing his few *reales* had been taken along with his clothes, and he could exchange the animal for food when he reached the next village. He hobbled it for the night, as he had seen the peons on the hacienda do with their burros, and lay down on the ground where he was, hungry, tired, and more than a little frightened.

He had hoped that in the morning some traveler would pass this way, someone to whom he could tell his story, someone who would be sympathetic and offer to help. But no one came from either direction. During the dark hours of the night he had decided to swallow his pride and return to Puebla, but with daylight he realized that it was impossible.

In such ragged, dirty clothes he would be refused entrance at Alejandro's front door. He would have to appeal to the servants, who would be loath to disturb their master. Then, if he finally succeeded in reaching his brother, town servants, unlike those on the hacienda, would talk. They would consider the whole thing a great joke and tell their friends, the servants of other creoles. Before he knew it, poor Alejandro would be the laughing stock of the countryside.

No, it would be far better to continue on to the city. Somehow he must gain the presence of the *Licenciado* Hidalgo and convince him that the ragged, dirty stranger was truly the son of his old friend Don Anselmo de Fuentes. The *licenciado* could send word to Alejandro, who would advance money for Nando's expenses, and the whole thing could be hushed up.

Remembering the bandit's sombrero, he tilted his own on the back of his head and started out on foot, leading the burro by its rope.

The forest seemed even more extensive than he

had been led to believe. The trees were oak, pine, and cedar, which had grown to such height that the road winding among them was in perpetual twilight. It was a steady climb, and before long Nando's tired legs forced him to ride on the burro rather than lead it. By now his stomach was so empty it was a constant pain. Hunger filled his thoughts so completely that when he finally emerged from the Black Forest he hardly noticed. But the burro knew and stopped short, letting the late sunlight warm through the rough coat.

They had reached the heights, and below was spread the great valley of Mexico. Nando strained his eyes to see. All his life he had heard stories of the conquest of the Aztecs by Cortez and his four hundred men, one of whom was his own ancestor. He knew that once Tenochtitlán, as Mexico City was called, was a great city of canals and lakes, pyramid-temples and palaces. He hadn't expected the pyramids to be there. After all, it was only proper that pagan symbols should be destroyed in favor of Christian churches. But surely some trace of the waterways must remain. There were none at all, at least none he could see from this distance. Oh, there was a little water, but only in the form of small lakes scattered haphazardly in the great basin. He thought he could make out cathedral spires clustered in the midst of the plain but he could not be sure. He was probably imagining them, for there was still a long way to go.

Impatiently he kicked at the burro's matted coat, but the animal refused to go on. It was the way of burros, Nando remembered, having seen such behavior in the animals belonging to the peons. He slid down and took the rope in his hand, hoping that the burro would proceed without a rider. To his great relief, it did.

The road descended abruptly and soon the country became barren and flat. There was a hint of the lakes which had once covered the land in a flight of water birds soaring upward from a marsh, although they only added to the bleakness of the landscape. But of even more immediate interest to Nando were the long, low adobe buildings on the right side of the road not over a mile distant. As he and the burro plodded wearily along, he could see that they comprised a rustic inn, nothing to commend itself to a luxury-demanding creole, but nothing had ever looked so inviting to Nando before. Here would be food to ease the throbbing in his stomach.

Before he reached them, however, he was startled by noises from behind. At first he was afraid it might be the bandits, and he gave a sigh of relief when he saw it was the *diligencia* from Puebla. He remembered that they had been scheduled to leave at three in the morning, stopping en route to change coach horses, and were expected to reach the city sometime after nightfall.

They made quite a stir advancing down the dusty road, a dozen or so horsemen astride weary mounts, including a few soldiers, and three cumbersome boxlike coaches, each drawn by eight horses. These swayed and tilted perilously, and as they drew closer Nando could hear the rattling and banging sounds which must have made conversation within impossible.

At first he stood where he was, stupidly holding on to the rope. But the burro was wiser than he and began tugging to get out of the way. Nando felt his cheeks burn. Naturally a ragged peon would hurry to clear the roadway for persons wealthy enough to employ the services of the *diligencia*. He let the burro lead him safely out of the path.

When the company had rattled and banged by, and after the dust had cleared away, Nando and the burro continued on. His forehead gathered in a frown when he saw that the *diligencia* had come to a stop in front of the inn, but there was nothing he could do about it.

They were still there when he arrived, and Nando could see laborers working over the wheel of one of the coaches. Something must have gone wrong, and it would have to be repaired before they could continue. He realized that he must wait until they had gone before attempting to sell the burro. The innkeeper would have his hands full with the rich ones.

Without thinking, he led his animal to the place where riding horses were tied. It did not occur to him to do anything else until he heard an angry voice shouting at him.

"Boy, who do you think you are? Get that burro away from the fine steeds of the gentlemen before I flay the skin from your body."

Hastily he pulled on the rope.

"I'm sorry," he mumbled, glancing over to the workman who had paused in his labors to do the shouting.

A plump, dignified gentleman, obviously a passenger in the coach, was standing beside the workman, asking questions. Next to him was a girl in a blue traveling dress. Reddish-brown hair hung below her blue bonnet, and from a face marred with a sprinkling of freckles, round gray eyes were regarding Nando with surprise. It was the girl he had seen outside the cathedral in Puebla, the one who had been laughing at him!

More embarrassed than ever, Nando jerked on the rope, almost pulling the surprised burro off balance in his efforts to get to the rear of the building.

A native boy had been left in charge of the stable, and he good-naturedly agreed that Nando might wait there with his burro until the *patrón* had time to talk.

"But if you wish to sell that one to the *patrón*," he added, jerking a dirty thumb in the direction of the burro and giving Nando a knowing grin, "you had better save your time. A man does not buy what belongs to him, and that burro was stolen from this stable less than a week ago."

Nando stared at the boy in horror. He should have known that an animal so freely given must come from near by and would be easily recognized. Then he saw the boy snatch his hat from his head and begin bowing, and at the same time he heard himself being addressed from the rear.

"Fernando de Fuentes, what are you doing here? And why are you masquerading in those clothes? Don't you know you have given your brother Don Alejandro a great fright? The whole city of Puebla is looking for you."

The girl had followed him around the corner of the building. She stood, her hands on her hips, regarding him with a deliberately forced frown, but Nando was unpleasantly aware that the gray eyes were dancing with mischief.

"Señorita, you have made a great mistake," he said quickly. "I am not Fernando de Fuentes. I am —I am Juan Sanchez."

"So?" She turned an imperial gaze on the gaping stable boy. "Leave us," she commanded. "Go far away. But stay well in sight so I may be sure you have not crept up to eavesdrop."

"As you say, señorita," agreed the boy, and trotted well back out of earshot where he stood staring with astonishment.

"Now," said the girl firmly. "You might as well admit who you are. I saw you at the cathedral. I watched you all during the mass, and I never forget a face. I am Isobel María Teresa Magdalena Rodriguez. I saw you jump on your black horse and ride away, and I knew that instant you were involved in some intrigue. I love intrigues. They are the most exciting things in all the world. I am involved in several at the present time, and you might as well tell me yours for I shall get it out of you sooner or later."

Nando drew a deep breath. The girl's words were spoken so rapidly that they had been difficult to follow, and they left him a little dizzy. She seemed to sense his difficulty for she smiled at him kindly.

"One thing at a time," she decided, tapping them off on her fingers. "You are Fernando de Fuentes?"

He nodded silently. There was nothing he could do but admit it.

"And you have run away from your brother Alejandro?" When he nodded once more, she smiled her approval. "I don't blame you. He is an indolent do-nothing. He is in love with my cousin Florinda Velarde. Perhaps you saw her at the cathedral? It would be a good match. She is as dull as he. We were visiting our cousins Don Dionisio Velarde and Doña Marilaria in Puebla, which is why we came to the mass. We are on our way home to San Miguel el Grande, where my father is *alcalde*. There are some fine intrigues in San Miguel. Where are you going?"

"To Mexico City."

"We will stop there, but for only a couple of days. Now, whom do you seek in Mexico City, dressed in this outlandish disguise?"

"The *Licenciado* Hidalgo," said Nando meekly. Answering this girl was like having lessons with his tutor. Somehow he felt required to give the correct answers.

"The *Licenciado* Hidalgo?" The smile widened across her face. "Now I begin to understand. I do not know him, although my father has a letter to him, so we will be calling. But I know his brother, Father Miguel Hidalgo. He is at Dolores. Perhaps you will be coming to Dolores?"

"Isobel!" Señor Rodriguez's horrified pink face appeared around the corner of the building. "What are you doing out here, conversing with the peons? What would your mama say? Come at once!"

"Yes, Papa," agreed Isobel instantly. Before she left she looked over her shoulder at Nando, winked one of the round eyes, and whispered, "Do not worry, Fernando. I will keep the secret of your intrigue. And we will meet again. I am sure of it."

After she had gone the stable boy returned, scratching his head with perplexity.

"What could that fine señorita have to say to one like you?"

"She mistook me for someone else," improvised Nando quickly. "She thought I was the son of a peon who once worked on her father's hacienda."

"A peon named—whatever it was she said? It had a high sound to it."

"A sad story," nodded Nando. "A creole and a beautiful *Indito*. You know how it goes. It could not last. Now about your *patrón*'s burro—"

"Of course. The stolen burro," remembered the boy, instantly diverted. "You are not trying to sell it?"

"I am returning it," explained Nando with dignity. "I found it wandering in the Black Forest."

"Ah?" The boy grinned knowingly. "My *patrón* is not one who parts lightly with silver for a reward, but perhaps a small meal—"

"It is more than enough," accepted Nando, rubbing his stomach.

"Then come with me," invited the boy. "We will go to the kitchen. The cook is my mother."

When the cook heard that Nando had returned a lost burro and was willing to be rewarded with a meal, she smiled and heaped a plate with beans and tortillas. From the glances she exchanged with her son, Nando was sure that the two of them would later claim a greater reward for the restoration of the animal, but he did not care.

He sat on the ground and devoured the food as fast as he could.

"How far to the city?" he asked between swallows.

"Afoot? Four hours, perhaps five."

"Could I stay here for the night? Sleep in the hay, perhaps?"

"No, no," cried the cook quickly, and Nando was more certain than ever that they meant to collect a reward for the burro. "The *patrón* would not permit it. You must go on. Now. As soon as you have eaten."

As he set out Nando could see that the workmen were fitting the wheel onto the coach. Soon the *diligencia* would be on its way. It would reach the city later that night, but Nando himself was too tired to walk that far. He would have to stop somewhere by the roadside and sleep.

In his mind he began considering the advisability of calling out to the *diligencia* as it passed. Isobel Rodriguez had recognized him. She could vouch for him, and when her parents realized that Nando was the brother of the suitor of their cousin, they would take pity on him. They would see that he had a place in the coach, suitable clothes, and somewhere to stay in the city. Then they would send word to Alejandro.

At that point his plans came to a definite halt. He could not do that to Alejandro. The *licenciado* was one matter, but relatives of the girl his brother hoped to marry were quite another. When he heard the *diligencia* rattling and banging behind him, he stood aside to let it pass.

5

"Candy! Fine candy of burnt milk, of cactus hearts, of sweet potatoes!" The vendor elbowed rudely against Nando, lowering his tray so that the boy might have a mouth-watering glimpse of the sweets. "Candy, *muchacho?* Finest candy in Mexico."

"No," said Nando regretfully, although once again his stomach was painfully empty.

He stood on the *zócalo*, the great square, of Mexico City, and all around him surged many hundreds of its residents. He had never seen anything to compare with it, and if he hadn't arrived as he had, in the ragged clothes of the lowest class, he never would have. If he had come as himself, as Fernando Genero Diego Rómolo de Fuentes, astride one of the splendid horses from the hacienda, the view would have been quite different. Then people would have moved back to make way, he told himself. They would not have dared to push and elbow, or even to ignore him. He felt very unclean and a little frightened, but he couldn't help appreciating the color and strangeness of his surroundings.

He was facing the great cathedral, which was even larger than the one in Puebla, with tall spires which surely must pierce the clouds on days when the sky hung low over the city. What a gigantic undertaking it must have been to erect such a church! Nando remembered hearing that it was built on the site of the great Aztec pyramid. Many of the pagan stones were used as the foundation for the Christian church.

On his right was the palace of the viceroys, a gray stone structure which lacked the graceful beauty of the cathedral. But his ancestor, the *Conquistador*, must have visited often within its walls, for portions of it had been built by Cortez, and for that reason Nando was inclined to be uncritical of its square, stark lines.

But most of all he looked at the crowd which surged about him. There were monks in long, dark habits; soldiers in uniforms of white and blue with billowing yellow capes; Indians, with woven *sarapes* thrown about their brown bodies, balancing jars of water or basins of grease on their bare heads; native

women with black *rebozos* over their even blacker
hair and bright-colored, dragging petticoats; half-
naked children; and above all, beggars.

Nando had never seen so many beggars before,
nor had he ever smelled anything to equal the odor
which clung to the rags with which they had
wrapped themselves. Many, he saw, were deformed,
and others pretended to be when they were not,
but almost every one was a *mestizo.* He remembered
Cardito's words, that there was little place in society for one of mixed blood and that there were
more *mestizos* in the country than anyone realized.
Truly Cardito had spoken with great wisdom, but
Nando wondered how he had known.

He had arrived in the city about noon and had
followed the crowds to the square. Now that he was
here, he was a little uncertain about what he should
do next. Naturally he must find the house of the
Licenciado Hidalgo, but which of these people could
he ask? For some reason, the streets seemed emptied
of the upper class, and who among this motley
crowd would know the residence of anyone so exalted as a *licenciado?* Unless— Of course! One of
the monks might be able to tell him.

There was a cluster of long-robed members of
the clergy standing in a little group just outside the
gates of the cathedral. Nando pushed his way ruth-
lessly through the throng, and when he drew nearer
he could see that they were overseeing the laying
of a heap of fagots. As he stared, two Indians ap-

proached, their backs bent under additional piles of sticks, which they dumped upon the others.

Nando removed his disreputable sombrero and held it before his breast as he neared the group.

"With your permission, Father," he said humbly, having selected the monk who seemed to wear the pleasantest expression.

He had made a good choice, for the man turned and his face crinkled into a merry smile.

"Yes, my son?"

"I am from Puebla," began Nando, for he was sure the monk would require some explanation before he would give out the address of so exalted a personage as the *licenciado*. "I have never been in this great city before, but I have a cousin who works here in the house of the *Licenciado* Hidalgo. I pray you, from the goodness of your heart, give me directions for finding that establishment so that I may join my cousin."

"To be sure, my son," cried the monk cordially. "You will go down that street, which is called the Calle de San Francisco. You will continue straight ahead past three crossings of other streets, then you will turn in that direction." A plump hand appeared from the black folds of the cassock to point south. "Continue on until you come to a gray wall over which you cannot see, but vines and flowering plants will peep down at you from the top."

"Yes, Father," agreed Nando carefully. "So far it is very clear."

"There is a door in the middle of the wall, and you will find a bell rope. Pull the rope. Someone will answer the door, whereupon you may give your name and ask for your cousin."

"A thousand thanks for your courtesy to a stranger, Father."

"But," the monk stopped him with a wave of his plump white hand, "do not be surprised if your cousin is not there. The *Licenciado* Hidalgo is a member of the *Inquisición*. He will doubtless have excused his servants to witness the burning."

"The burning, Father?"

"The burning of the heretic. Right here." The monk made a smiling gesture toward the steadily increasing pile of fagots. "It will take place later this afternoon."

"Perhaps if I go now I can catch my cousin before he leaves," mumbled Nando, growing cold with horror.

"Perhaps," smiled the monk. "Then you can return together. Go with God, my son."

Nando hurried away across the square, which was the termination of the Street of San Francisco. No wonder there were so few upper class visitors to the *zócalo*. The last thing he himself wanted to see was the public burning of a heretic. That, however, was the usual punishment imposed by the *Inquisición*, a body of churchmen who were appointed to look into these matters. The *Inquisición* was a fearful thing and was especially active in the cities. Its long arm did not reach into the distant provinces quite so often.

Following the monk's instruction, he turned off the Calle de San Francisco at the third crossing and followed a quieter street. When he came to the gray wall he looked up to make sure that flowering vines were visible over the top. He couldn't miss them; pink geranium, wine-red bougainvillea, and white star flowers had climbed as high as they could go and were spilling over the side.

When he found the door Nando pulled the rope, listening to make sure that the bell rang within the walls. As he prepared to wait, he tilted his sombrero well back on his head. Here, of all places, he must convince people of his honesty.

There was no answer, so after a proper interval he pulled the rope again, and finally a third time. Eventually he heard the rasp of an iron bar, and the upper half of the door swung back. An old man with a seamed brown face and gray hair hanging untidily about his neck stared out at him.

"Who are you? What do you want?"

"I wish to see the *Licenciado* Hidalgo. I am the son of one of his oldest friends." Nando drew himself up proudly, hoping that his manner would offset his bedraggled appearance.

"It is not wise to make the joke here," the old man told him angrily. "The *licenciado* is a great man. His friends are great men. They do not have sons like you. Anyway," he concluded before slam-

ming the door, "if you were the son of the king of
Spain you could not see the *licenciado* now. It is the
siesta."

The *siesta,* of course. How stupid he had been not
to remember that this was the hour when all of
Mexico rested. Why even the peons on the Hacienda
del Fuentes were allowed their time of relaxation
in the heat of the day. When they awoke they could
work twice as hard to make up for it. Nando's world
had been turned so upside down that the routine
things of life were forgotten.

There was nothing to do now but wait, and it was
far better to wait here than to go back to the *zócalo,*
where the *Inquisición* was about to exact its terrible
punishment. Nando sat down on the cobblestones,
his back next to the wall, and pulled his sombrero
over his face. The sun felt warm on his body, and
the flowers scented the air. Before he knew it he was
asleep.

He awoke to the sound of horses' hooves on the
cobbled streets and to the rumbling and bumping
of a coach. He sat up, pushing back the sombrero.
For a moment he could not remember where he
was. Then it all came back to him, and as he saw
the horses come to a stop before the wide door in
the wall, he realized that this was his opportunity.

The footman climbed down and rang the bell.
When the gate was opened the coachman drove
through and Nando slipped in beside it. He was
careful to keep the coach between himself and the

gatekeeper, hoping frantically that the passengers would not look out of the window and see him trotting alongside.

The driveway circled through a beautiful garden filled with fountains and luxurious shrubs. Nando selected a particularly thick flowering stand within sight of the arched façade leading to the house and dropped off behind it. He must wait there patiently until the callers had gone before attempting to see the *licenciado*. The fewer people who knew about his predicament the better.

Again the footman dismounted and opened the door for the passengers. Nando caught his breath. It was the Rodriguez family! First came Isobel's father, the pink-cheeked *alcalde*, who looked for all the world like a fat little pigeon in his gray velvet jacket and black trousers, then the equally plump señora, followed by Isobel herself, with her reddish-brown braids glistening in the sunlight.

As they entered the house, Nando remembered that the girl had mentioned they were to deliver a letter from Hidalgo's brother, the *cura* of some little town near their home. It was only natural that they would present it as soon as possible.

Mexican visits could be of an indeterminate length. Nando had known callers to stay as long as four or five hours, even stopping on to take dinner with their hosts. So he was greatly surprised when the Rodriguezes reappeared in less than thirty minutes. A distinguished gentleman of middle age, wearing the rich clothing of a creole, walked with them to their carriage. He bowed over the señora's and Isobel's hands, saluted the *alcalde,* and stood politely waiting until they had driven away. As he prepared to return to the house, Nando jumped from his hiding place.

"Señor *Licenciado,* please. One moment!"

Hidalgo stopped, frowning at the ragged figure which had been concealed in his shrubbery.

"Juan," he called sharply. "Pablo!"

Immediately two servants trotted from the house to take their stands beside their master.

"Señor, do not be afraid. And please forgive me for appearing thus. There was no other way to gain your august presence," cried Nando anxiously. He was uncomfortably aware of the appearance he was making, but somehow he must make this man believe him.

"Well," demanded the *licenciado* sharply.

"I know I don't look it, but I am Fernando Genero Diego Rómolo de Fuentes, son of your old friend Don Anselmo de Fuentes. You do remember Don Anselmo, señor?"

"Perfectly," said the *licenciado* coldly. "Don Anselmo is a fine creole gentleman. In his veins runs the blood of the *Conquistadores.* You do him insult by claiming to be his son. Throw him out."

This last remark was addressed to Juan and Pablo, who obeyed without hesitation. Nando felt himself being lifted bodily from his feet and carried from the garden.

"But I can explain," he cried over his shoulder. "Send a message to my brother Alejandro at Puebla de los Angeles. Please wait."

But Juan and Pablo did not wait. Someone opened the door, and together they gave Nando a rousing swing which landed him outside on the cobblestoned street.

For a moment he lay there trying to catch his breath; then he saw the approaching horses. They were almost upon him before the coachman noticed him in the street and pulled them to a halt.

Nando staggered to his feet, reeling. A moment later he heard a girl's shrill voice calling from the coach.

"Why, Nando, you naughty, naughty boy! What are you doing here? Why aren't you back in Dolores where you belong? Whatever will Father Hidalgo say?"

Without waiting for the footman, Isobel opened the coach door and jumped down. Lifting her long skirts, she ran over to Nando and leaned close to whisper her instructions.

"Leave everything to me. Do not say a word, only nod."

Her gray eyes had been sparkling with excitement, but as she turned back to the coach the gleam was gone, swallowed in a proper look of indignation.

"You see, Papa. You see, Mama. It is as we were saying. The *Licenciado* Hidalgo is not like his brother, the *cura*, at all. He has no heart, this one. He will not even give assistance to one who has made a long, wearisome pilgrimage for the sake of Our Lady."

"Isobel!" cried her mother, leaning from the coach, her scandalized brown eyes almost popping from her head. "Get back here this instant. Don Serapio, will you kindly order your daughter into the coach?"

The *alcalde*'s round, pink face appeared beside that of his wife in the window.

"Isobel! You heard your mama."

"But we must help," explained Isobel. "In Christian charity we must give aid to this poor boy."

"He is only a peon." Don Serapio's small nose wrinkled with distaste. "And a dirty one at that! This is the second time in two days, Doña Triumfa, that I have found your daughter interesting herself in the welfare of a peon," he added accusingly to his wife.

"Please tell them who I am, señorita," begged Nando wearily. There was no other way out. These cousins of Alejandro's betrothed would have to know the truth.

"Of course I will tell, you poor, poor boy," promised Isobel, her voice ringing with pity. She turned to her parents and her sad smile begged for their understanding. "This is Nando. He has no other name, or if he has one I have never heard it. He is the most trusted servant and pupil of Father Hidalgo."

"Of *our* Father Hidalgo?" asked Doña Triumfa in surprise. "Father Hidalgo of Dolores?"

"Who else?" Isobel sighed and shrugged her shoulders helplessly. "Nando is one of great piety. On foot he came all the distance from Dolores to the Shrine of Our Lady of Guadalupe. You can see for yourself by his ragged clothing—he who is ordinarily so neat and clean—that it was a difficult journey."

"It is a long way from Dolores to the Shrine of Our Lady," said Don Serapio reluctantly.

"But not so far from her shrine to the City of Mexico," his daughter reminded him quickly. "After he made his pilgrimage, what would be more natural for the beloved pupil of Father Hidalgo than to call on his *patrón's* brother, the *licenciado?* And you can see for yourself how he was received! He was thrown into the street!"

"But how do you know this was the case, Isobel," asked Don Serapio doubtfully. "How can you know?"

"Did you not, with your own eyes, see him thrown bodily from the doorway?" demanded Isobel indignantly. "Was that not so, Nando? Is it not true that when you endeavored to speak with the *licenciado*, he had you thrown from his premises?"

"Yes, señorita," agreed Nando helplessly. "But—"

"As for the beginning of his story, I have just

told it to you," Isobel reminded her parents. "I can vouch for it. I, myself, have seen him with the *cura*. I, myself, have heard of his brilliance as a pupil. I, myself, was aware of his intention to make this pilgrimage to the shrine. What further proof can you ask?"

"Well, well," said the *alcalde* feebly. "It is too bad you have been received thus. But perhaps if you had not been so dirty—if your clothing was not so ragged—"

"Señor, will you permit me to explain about my clothing?" begged Nando.

"There is no need," declared Isobel. "The finest raiment would become soiled on the long journey from Dolores to Mexico City. Even in a coach it would become soiled. Think then how much dirtier it would become if one was so pious as to make the trip on foot."

"True," agreed Don Serapio thoughtfully. "It would gather much dust."

"Now we must decide what we are to do. We must think what Father Hidalgo would expect of us, his friends," insisted Isobel firmly.

"First we must recover my gloves," remembered Doña Triumfa. "My new gloves, which I was stupid enough to forget during the call. I can purchase none like them in San Miguel el Grande, and I must have them. That is, after all, why we returned to the house of the *licenciado*, to recover my gloves."

"Ring the bell," ordered Don Serapio quickly. He

looked up through the window at the high seat outside of the coach, and the footman immediately
climbed down, crossed over to the door, and rang
the bell.

"There is only one thing to do," said Isobel, frowning at the interruption. "Tomorrow we must take
Father Hidalgo's pupil back with us to San Miguel
el Grande. From there he can reach Dolores quite
easily."

"He came on foot," remembered Doña Triumfa.
"And the coach is crowded. There are two on the
high seat now. It does not hold three."

"Your mama is right," declared Don Serapio. "He
cannot ride inside with us. Even Father Hidalgo
would not expect Christian charity to extend so
far."

Isobel bit her lip.

"Then he can ride on the step," she declared after
a moment. "It may be bumpy, but it's better than
walking."

"Señorita, please," cried Nando imploringly. He
had never met such a girl. Lies fell from her lips
like water from a downspout after a hard rain. Girls
were supposed to be demure and modest, with
downcast eyes and few words. This girl had an
inexhaustible supply of words, and they welled up
and spilled over to make room for others. How
could her parents permit such behavior? How could
they believe such a story as she had just concocted
out of nothing? And yet, it was a credible story. It

could have happened to someone, only it hadn't happened to him. The things which had happened to him were even more unbelievable.

"I imagine it will not be too comfortable on the step, Nando," said Isobel graciously. "You will have to hold on very tightly, for I fear the road is filled with ruts. But you will admit that it is better than walking?"

"Yes, señorita, it would be better than walking," Nando gulped a little. "However, if the coach does not go in the direction one wishes to take—"

"Oh, as for that, you will have to be patient until morning." Isobel smiled tolerantly. "We start for San Miguel el Grande very early, eh, Papa?"

"Very early, *chica*," Don Serapio beamed at his daughter fondly. "Before daybreak."

"Tonight you will have to remain at the inn where we are staying. I am sure there will be a place for you to sleep in the hay. You will not mind the hay, Nando. It was the first cradle of the Blessed Jesus, you remember. You can practice riding on the step while we drive there now. We will arrive just in time for dinner."

Dinner! Nando involuntarily passed a hand over his flat stomach. Yes, he would go with the Rodriguez family to their inn. He would gladly eat the food they provided, perhaps he might even pass the night in the stable. But tomorrow—well, tomorrow would have to take care of itself.

"Ay, my gloves," announced Doña Triumfa with

satisfaction as she saw the gatekeeper pass something through the doorway to the waiting footman. "Now we can go."

Nando settled himself on the high step outside the coach door. It was not wide, but he could hang on to the brace. As the horses started ahead, pulling the cumbersome vehicle, he felt his teeth rattling together with the vibration. Well, the inn could not be too far distant, he consoled himself. He could stand it for a little while.

6

The dinner at the inn was good. If this was the fare provided for the servants, thought Nando to himself, the dishes served to the first class guests must be superb. Someday, when he was himself, one of the young masters of the Hacienda del Fuentes, he would come here again for a real treat. And then he remembered that at the rate he was going he would be lucky if he even managed to become a *cura* of the smallest, most humble parish in a distant province.

As a member of the retinue of the Rodriguez family, there was no question but that he would be permitted to spend the night in the stables. He had gone there after supper to inspect the cleanliness of the hay, hoping for the best but prepared for anything, when he was sought out by one of the *criadas*, a maid, employed by the inn. The Señorita Rodriguez wished to speak to him immediately.

"Where is the señorita?" asked Nando, a little suspiciously. He felt well fed and almost comfortable, and Isobel Rodriguez had proved herself to be a most disquieting individual. "Do I go to the salon?"

"Oh no," giggled the maid. "The señorita has secreted herself behind a bush just outside the kitchen door. She is a sly one, the señorita. Her mama thinks she has gone to her room with a headache. She gave me a *peseta* to find you and bring you to her. Whatever can she want with the likes of you?" she added curiously.

"Perhaps she wishes me to deliver a message to someone," suggested Nando frowning. After all, Isobel was a creole like himself. It was not proper for one of the *Indios* to be whispering that she was odd.

"Doubtless." The girl seemed satisfied with the explanation. "But she is young to be sending secret messages."

She pointed out the bush and Nando went there immediately. Isobel had tucked up her long skirts and was sitting on the ground in the shadows away from the light which came from the open door. She had been contemplating the stars, and as Nando arrived she gestured skyward with a jerk of her head.

"Father Hidalgo can tell you about them. He knows many of them by name. He knows everything."

"That's nice," growled Nando. He knew she hadn't summoned him here to talk about the stars, and he had no wish to talk about her precious Father Hidalgo. The *Licenciado* Hidalgo had been quite enough.

"It is time that you told me about your intrigue." Isobel got down to business at once. "Or at least what you thought was going to be an intrigue. Obviously it failed."

Nando sighed. He would have to tell her some of his problems anyway. And perhaps he did owe the girl something for providing him with dinner.

"I was going to come to Mexico City with the *diligencia* the day after the mass," he explained reluctantly. "I was going to study for the priesthood. Alejandro had written a letter to the *licenciado* asking him to help me. Only I decided not to wait. I came right from the cathedral, and I was attacked by bandits. They stole my horse and my clothes. These clothes belonged to a robber boy. I had to wear them because I didn't have any others. And since I didn't have the letter, the *licenciado* didn't believe who I was. He threw me out. That's all there is to it. There's no—what you call intrigue, at all."

To his surprise she did not challenge his last statement, nor did she seem disappointed.

"Do you really want to be a priest?" she asked curiously. "Have you wanted to for a long time?"

"No," admitted Nando honestly. "I hadn't even thought about it. But when my father died, Alejandro thought it would be best."

"Alejandro thought!" mimicked Isobel. She made a little face. Then she added shrewdly, "Why did you decide to leave so suddenly?"

"I just decided to, that's all."

"It was because you look like an Indian, wasn't it?" She leaned closer, her face peering up through the twilight, daring him to deny it. "Alejandro was ashamed of you, and that's why you ran away."

Nando said nothing. She had guessed his secret, but it was very rude of her to put it into words.

"There's nothing to be ashamed of," declared Isobel after a moment. "Half the creole families in Mexico have Indian blood. Everybody knows it, but they spend most of their time trying to prove that it isn't so. I personally think it's very silly of them."

"Is it true of you?" Since Isobel was so rude herself, Nando might as well be rude, too.

"I don't think so." She considered the matter a moment before she answered. "We haven't been here that long. My grandfather was a *gachupín*. He came from Madrid. My father is the first creole. Sometimes I think I might have been more beautiful if I did have a little of the Indian in me. Then I wouldn't have to be so smart."

"More beautiful if you were a *mestizo?*" gasped Nando.

"At least I wouldn't have freckles." Isobel seemed to realize that the conversation was getting out of bounds. She changed the subject abruptly. "Well, I can see why you don't want to go back to Puebla. I wouldn't want to go where people were ashamed of me, either."

"No," agreed Nando sadly. "But I'll have to let Alejandro know where I am so he can send the money. I can't go to school without money. And if I'm to be a priest—"

"You could go in the Army." Isobel's eyes sparkled in the starlight. "The Army is full of intrigues."

"It takes money to buy a commission," he reminded her. "Besides thirteen is too young."

"I suppose so." Again she made a little face. "It's very upsetting the way people go around saying you're too young for this and too young for that, isn't it? I don't think age is important. It's how you feel inside." After a moment she decided, "I guess it will have to be the church, although I don't think you should ask Alejandro for the money. Not just yet, anyway. Let him worry awhile. It will do him good."

"But how can I go to school, how can I study, without money?"

"That's simple." Isobel clasped her hands around

her knees and smiled widely. "I've thought it all out. You'll live with Father Hidalgo at Dolores. You'll study with him."

"But why should he help me when his brother wouldn't?"

"I'm afraid we'll have to tell him the truth," admitted Isobel regretfully. "But he'll listen. I promise you he will."

"It's silly to go all the way to Dolores," sputtered Nando angrily. "You know who I am. You could tell the *licenciado* or your parents. They'd believe you."

"Of course they would," agreed Isobel sweetly. She stood up. "But I won't tell them. I won't tell anyone who you are until we get to Dolores. Then I'll tell Father Hidalgo."

"What if I won't go?" Nando had never felt quite so frustrated in his life. He wanted to hit out at this girl, force her to tell the truth. Only, of course, no creole would ever do that.

"I suppose you could go crawling back to Alejandro," taunted Isobel. "It would make a fine story to tell in Puebla. Everyone's wondering what happened to you anyway, so they'd like to know. They would laugh and laugh, at you and Alejandro both. Otherwise, you can be on the step of our coach when we leave tomorrow morning."

Without waiting for a reply, she turned and circled the bush, entering the inn by way of the kitchen door.

Nando thought about the problem off and on all night. He slept fitfully, awakening from nightmares in which he was being alternately chased by bandits and being thrown out of the *licenciado*'s garden. The most terrible dream of all took place in the cathedral at Puebla. Alejandro was there, and Ramón, and Ramón's friend Captain Allende. They had gone together to mass, only when they arrived the others wouldn't let Nando sit with them. He had to kneel on the marble floor with the *Indios*, and most of them proved to be beggars from the *zócalo* in Mexico City. They didn't want him either. They kept trying to make him go back with his own family.

It was a dreadful night, and when the footman kicked him awake and told him the Rodriguez coach was making ready to start for San Miguel el Grande, Nando got up from the hay and stood meekly by the step waiting for the family to climb inside.

San Miguel was in the province of Guanajuato, the coachman told him when they made a breakfast stop at a wayside inn about nine o'clock. Like Mexico City, it was high in elevation. The air was very fine and clear, the country very beautiful. They must go north and west a long way to reach there, and the trip would take several days.

Several days! thought Nando in dismay, chewing on the tortilla he had been given. Each mile was taking him farther and farther from Puebla and the Hacienda del Fuentes. Was he out of his head?

Why was he doing this thing? He had much better confront Isobel in the presence of her parents right now and demand that she tell the truth. But he knew that she wouldn't tell. She would only lie. And what could he do then? He would be even worse off than before. Glumly he finished his tortilla, and when it was time to start he climbed back on the coach step.

By evening he was so bruised and sore from being bounced around, and his hands were so numb from holding on to the brace, that it was all he could do to swallow his supper. Isobel must have realized something of what he was going through for she found a moment to speak to him privately.

"I know it is very hard," she said sympathetically. "But it will be worth it later on. Remember I told you there were intrigues going on in San Miguel el Grande? We're going to have a part of them, you and I. I have it all planned."

Nando could only look at her weakly and make his way to the shed where he had been told he was to sleep that night.

The second day was a repetition of the first, but by the third Nando's muscles began to adjust themselves to the strain. At least his body didn't ache so much, and calluses were forming on his hands. They arrived in late afternoon at the city of Querétaro, and once again Isobel had a whispered communication for him.

"Keep your eyes open. Listen, and remember everything you hear. It may be important."

"Important to what?" asked Nando.

"I don't know." She frowned with annoyance. "I've already told you I don't know much about this intrigue. But I mean to find out. The house where we are staying belongs to my father's friend, the *corregidor* of Querétaro, Don Miguel Dominguez. He and his wife, Doña Josefa, are part of the intrigue. I'm sure of it."

"How can you be sure?"

"I just am," she insisted irritably. "Also the *alcalde*, Señor Perez. I think he knows about it, too."

"Is your father part of—whatever it is?" asked Nando curiously.

"Don't be stupid." Isobel looked at him with pity. "My father is a dear, sweet man. But you can tell just by looking at him that he wouldn't know an intrigue from a mousetrap."

"Probably not," agreed Nando. He had no idea what Isobel expected of him. He was doubtful that he himself would recognize whatever she called an intrigue if he met one, either. But he obligingly listened to the conversations of the servants, and was not surprised when they proved to be quite ordinary.

Early the next morning they set out on the final stage of their journey and arrived at San Miguel el Grande in late afternoon, just as the grackles were soaring into their nesting places among the trees in the square. Nando looked about him curiously as the carriage rattled and bounced over the cobblestones which paved the narrow streets.

Originally the town lay at the base of a steeply rising hill, but it had grown and now crawled up the eastern slope. There the walls seemed to cling precariously, and even tilt a little with the terrain, while the narrow winding streets between had sprung up from necessity, not by plan.

It was typical of most towns built by the Spaniards in their colonies, and the coach was traveling now between rows of high adobe walls tinted pink or white, blue or yellow. In most cases these outer walls comprised one side of the living quarters of the household and formed one support for the flat roofs. One long wall extended the entire length of every block, but was marked by many wooden doors, each leading to a private household. When some careless person had failed to close one of the doors, Nando had a glimpse into a flowered garden concealed within, for who is too poor to afford flowers?

In the first section the walls were no more than ten or twelve feet high, but as they approached the central square, they extended upward two or three stories. Here they were no longer made of adobe, but built of stone, flush with the street. Technically, they could no longer be called walls, either, for their stone faces were broken by windows latticed with ornamental iron work, and on the upper stories there were balconies which overhung the street. The doors were usually recessed, and always ornamented with carving.

Nando was not surprised when the carriage stopped before one of the carved doors. At the top two stone cherubs looked down upon any who crossed the sill. The *alcalde* would live in a fine house, he decided.

Obviously the horses were stabled at another place, and the carriage was summoned as it was needed, for the footman jumped down, rang the bell rope, and hurried back to assist the passengers.

Nando stood aside, awaiting orders, for he was quite sure Isobel would not forget him. As he glanced down the street, he saw a small company of mounted soldiers turn the corner and start toward them. When they reached the carriage, the captain in the lead lifted his hand, bringing his men to a halt.

Nando was puzzled. Although the street was narrow, two carriages could have squeezed through. A line of horsemen would have had no trouble passing on the other side of the coach. Then he saw that the captain was dismounting. A moment later he hurried forward to greet the Rodriguez family as they stood there at their doorway.

Nando gave a little gasp. The captain, bowing over the hand of Isobel's mother, Doña Triumfa, was Ramón's friend, Don Ignacio Allende.

7

Isobel was angry. Her gray eyes flashed, and the freckles stood out on her round face, which was flooded with unusual color.

"My mama!" she sputtered, glaring at Nando as though he might be in some way to blame. "She is stubborn. She is adamant. She will not be persuaded, although I even cried tears in an effort to move her. And Papa, he will not listen either. Oh, why did the good God make me a girl? Surely it was an unfortunate error. He meant me to be a boy."

Nando stared at her blankly. He supposed that eventually Isobel Rodriguez would explain the cause of her wrath, but until she was ready there was nothing to do but wait.

It was early morning. In the small back patio of the Rodriguez household, the one which was reserved for the use of the servants, the dew still clung to the pepper vines and to the pink geraniums which climbed up the sides of the back wall. The dew had been unusually heavy last night, a sure sign that before long the month of June, which ushered in the rainy season, would be upon them.

Isobel's initial outburst was now over, and her round face assumed an expression of deep concentration.

"I have arranged everything," she declared. "It would be better if I—but no, I must not even think of that. Mama says I cannot accompany you to Dolores, and so I must obey. There may occur another, more important, occasion when I will have to go against her wishes, and it is better that I give in this time."

So that was it. Doña Triumfa would not permit her daughter to make the last stage of the journey to find Father Hidalgo. Well, it was only natural. Why should a well-bred young creole need to accompany a peon who was supposed to know the country anyway? But Nando's heart grew heavy with foreboding. Father Hidalgo would probably throw him into the street as had his brother.

"I have written a letter." From somewhere in her dress Isobel produced a paper sealed with wax.

"Give it to Father Hidalgo, and let him read it before you say a word. After that everything will go well, and you will be ready for the important matters."

"Important matters?" repeated Nando.

"The intrigue!" Isobel frowned at his density. "I know that the *cura* is involved someway. I just know it. He might even be the head of it. Anyone so brilliant could very well be. The *Corregidor* Miguel Dominguez and his wife, the Doña Josefa, are in it, too. They must be, because most of the meetings are held in Querétaro. Harmless, literary society meetings they are called, and for some they are doubtless harmless. My own father, that innocent lamb, attends these meetings from time to time. But he knows nothing. I am sure of that. Whatever is said there must have a double meaning, and Papa hears but one."

"You want me to be a spy?" gasped Nando in horror.

"That is a poor word!" Isobel's pale eyebrows lifted and she drew herself up haughtily. Then her shoulders sagged and her tone grew coaxing. "If I had only been born a boy, I would not have to ask help from an outsider. Girls are restrained by foolish custom from going many interesting places. And I do want to know what's going on. I wouldn't try to stop it. I know that whatever it is is honorable. It couldn't be otherwise, not with people like Father Hidalgo and Doña Josefa involved. But it isn't fair of them to keep things to themselves. Not when I'm so good at intrigues."

Nando stared at her in amazement. Was it possible that this girl had gone to all this trouble to get him here just because of her great curiosity? Then, as he realized exactly what she was asking of him, he was filled with blazing anger.

"You are a snoop!" he accused hotly. "A busybody. A stick-your-nose-into-other-people's-business girl. You are— Oh, I can't think of anything bad enough to call you!"

"I know," agreed Isobel pleasantly. "But I wouldn't be if they didn't try to keep secrets. If they'd come out in the open and say what goes on at their precious little meetings I wouldn't even be interested."

"You could ask your papa."

"I have," she told him promptly. "He says they talk about books they have read. And because Papa doesn't read any books, he says he falls asleep so they won't call on him."

"Then why does he go?" demanded Nando suspiciously.

"He says it is so nice and quiet at the meetings," reported Isobel sadly. "Of course, what he really means is that Mama isn't there, always telling him to get up and do something for her. Fetch her fan or her shawl. Things like that. Besides, it's *the* thing to belong. A great many of our best people do."

"Oh," said Nando feeling relieved. "Then they wouldn't let me go to their meetings."

"You're too young, anyway," said Isobel. "But you can listen. Maybe you can overhear conversations. Remember every little thing you hear, so you can tell me later. I'm very good at piecing bits together."

Nando did not answer. He could only look at her. Even if he were accepted for a time in Father Hidalgo's household, he was sure he would not hear anything to interest Isobel.

"The Army is sending a packtrain of burros to Dolores this morning," she continued, accepting his silence as a consent to her schemes. "I heard about it from Captain Allende last night when he came in to pay his respects on our return. I've arranged for you to go with them."

Nando felt his cheeks begin to burn. Ramón's friend Don Ignacio Allende had not given a second glance to the tattered, dust-covered boy who jumped from the coach step and stood back while the family entered the house. But Nando knew there would be another meeting, and as yet he hadn't decided what to do about it. He could throw himself on Don Ignacio's mercy, and for Ramón's sake he was sure that the young creole would restore him to his former place in society. But would he want to? It was one thing to be gracious and friendly to a younger brother on the hacienda. But this was Allende's own territory. Obviously he was stationed here. Would it be right to embarrass him before his own friends? Nando couldn't make up his mind.

"At least Mamacita has agreed to loan you a burro," remembered Isobel. "You will not have to walk the twenty miles to Dolores."

At that very moment one of the stable boys appeared with the announcement that the burro ordered by the señorita was at the door. And just in time, too, for the packtrain from the garrison was already crossing the square.

"You have the letter?" Isobel's eyes sparkled. "Remember carefully everything that I have told you. And when Father Hidalgo comes the next time to San Miguel el Grande, be sure to accompany him. For, as you see, it is difficult for me to go there. Now, go with God."

Almost before he knew it Nando was hustled from the patio and out into the street. As the door slammed shut behind him his eyes fell on the burro standing just before the door, vainly attempting to extract a few wisps of herbage which had struggled up between the stones. The next moment the packtrain had rounded the corner and was coming toward him.

There were four burros in the train, each bearing a pack almost as big as the animal's body. They were headed by a *mestizo*, who wore the uniform of a noncommissioned officer and was astride a mule. An Indian private brought up the rear on foot, and it was obviously his duty to keep any stragglers on the move. As they reached the Rodriguez doorway, the leader halted his mule and stared down at Nando curiously.

"You are the one attached to the household of Father Hidalgo?"

Nando nodded silently, and the man shook his head in amazement.

"You do not appear of such great worth as to merit an escort. But they have given you a burro to ride, so there must be more than meets the eye. Fall in behind."

Nando waited until they had moved ahead, then he took the burro's rope in his hand and followed. After the *mestizo's* critical stare he felt a little self-conscious about mounting the animal.

It was a wise decision, for being on foot put him on a friendly level with the Indian, who immediately waited so they could walk together.

"I am Jesús Ferías." He smiled, showing a wide gap in his mouth where some teeth were missing.

"I am Fernando de Fuentes." Courtesy demanded that he give his own name once a stranger had stated his, and Nando had decided he might as well start telling the truth. Father Hidalgo would know as soon as he read Isobel's letter, and before long Ramón's friend Captain Ignacio Allende would know, too. He smiled at the soldier, realizing that this was his opportunity to find out about the captain's presence in San Miguel el Grande. He had many questions which he had been afraid to put to Isobel.

"It must be very fine to be a soldier," he began slyly. "Have you been here at this garrison long?"

"Almost a year now." The man's chest swelled with pride under Nando's evident admiration. "You are correct. There are times when it is a good life. Other times, like now, when I must walk the long, dusty way to Dolores as though I were a common peon, I do not find so good."

"Is your commander a good man? Is he just?" asked Nando carefully. "I saw him last night. Captain Allende, if I heard his name correctly. He is very handsome in his fine uniform."

"Yes, he is a good man," declared the soldier promptly. "And just, too, although he is sometimes too concerned with matters which have small meaning. When we go on parade, for instance, every man must wash his hands and face. Would you believe it? And his hair must be smoothed just so, and his hat placed on his head at a certain slant. In these little matters, small things which should be of no concern to a fighting man, he is too particular. But he is a good commander. Very brave. Very wise."

"He has been at this garrison a long time?"

"He was here when I came," remembered Jesús thoughtfully. "I have heard that once he was with General Calleja. They say he was with a regiment of dragoons."

"The Queen's Regiment," supplied Nando without thinking, then could have bitten his own tongue.

But Jesús did not seem to think it strange a ragged peon should know such military details.

"You have heard of it," he approved. "It was, I believe, at San Luis Potosí—or maybe somewhere else. But San Miguel el Grande is the captain's native city. He was born here, and now lives in the same house. It is at the west corner of the square, a fine, stone house, although I have never been inside, of course. It is only natural that he should ask to be returned to this place, where he can also keep an eye on his business."

"His business?"

"He possesses a tannery for the preparation of hides into leather," Jesús told him, smiling. "Of course, the captain himself has nothing to do with it. But the revenues—ah, that is another matter."

"Of course," agreed Nando. There was still one more question which he wanted to ask, which he had to ask. He was almost afraid to put it into words, and yet he had to know. "Did you ever hear of an officer with the same name as mine, de Fuentes?" he said bravely. "Perhaps a friend of your captain?"

Jesús laughed merrily.

"No, boy." He winked tears of mirth from his eyes, leaving little smudges along his dusty cheeks. "It is a name I have never heard before today, when you told me it was yours. I see what you have in mind. Someday, when you are older, if you are lucky, you wish to join the Army. But you will be a private like me. The officers are only the great ones, creoles and *gachupines*."

Jesús proved to be a most agreeable companion and guide and showed Nando all the spots of interest along the way. He pointed out the sanctuary of Atotonilco, only a short distance from San Miguel, a very holy place indeed, almost as holy as the Shrine of Guadalupe. It was not so tall as the cathedrals in Mexico City or Puebla, but it spread itself over a large expanse of dry, sun-baked ground, and the great tiled dome between two towers was festooned today with garlands, brought by some pious pilgrim and hung there at peril to his life. Jesús said that this was a place of retreat, where pilgrims came to pray and where they castigated themselves with cruel whips and wore crowns made of thorns.

"Is there some special saint for the sanctuary?" asked Nando curiously.

Jesús scratched his head and said that he did not think so.

"But there is a great banner of the Virgin inside," he remembered. "Very fine. Very magnificent. It is almost like the original, which hangs in the Virgin of Guadalupe's shrine."

The day was warm and the twenty miles were long behind the slow-moving packtrain. In exchange for the soldier's freely given friendship, Nando invited him to share the burro provided by Isobel Rodriguez. The two of them took turns riding, and their laughter and conversation made the *mestizo* leader turn often on his mule and look back at them with astonishment.

In midafternoon they arrived at the outskirts of Dolores and Nando began to grow nervous. In the company of Jesús Ferías, he had almost forgotten that he would soon be faced by another member of the Hidalgo family.

Dolores was a poor town and had none of the pretentious homes of San Miguel el Grande. The creoles in the vicinity preferred to live on nearby haciendas, and since it was their money which erected elaborate buildings, those of Dolores huddled like squat yellow ducks on the sere brown plain. People lived behind walls, of course, but there was no money to buy paint for the adobe, so the walls had a monotonous sameness, and even the trees which peered over from a few enclosed patios looked parched and dry.

Jesús, who had been the last to ride the burro, jumped off suddenly and grinned.

"Well, here you are, Fernando," he announced. "Your presence has made the day more enjoyable, for which I give you thanks."

Nando took the burro's rope, which the soldier thrust into his hands, and stood staring stupidly.

"Your house," said Jesús, lifting his eyebrows in surprise and gesturing toward the yellow wall before him. "The house of the *cura* of Dolores. It is here you leave us, is it not?"

"Of course," agreed Nando quickly. "Go with God, and thank you."

"For nothing," answered Jesús politely, and trotted off after his charges.

Staring at the sand-colored adobe, Nando realized that this was more than a wall with an entrance door. Although it was but one story in height, there were three windows barred with iron, and a lamp with a space for a candle within the glass hung above the door. But there was no carving, no plaster figures to show that this was the residence of a man of the cloth, and certainly no more paint than on the neighboring houses.

He tilted his sombrero to show his honesty and pulled on the rope. From within he heard the metallic sounds as the iron clapper struck against the sides of the bell, and after a few moments the plain wooden door was opened.

"You have come to see the *cura?*" asked a very old woman, whose face was etched with so many wrinkles that it was almost impossible to imagine what she must have looked like when she was young. Her gray hair was neatly braided into one long tail, which hung down her stooped back, and her long cotton dress was clean, although well mended.

"Please to enter," she invited when Nando nodded bashfully. As he motioned toward the burro, which stood at the doorway, she lifted her voice and called, "Carlos, come!"

In a moment or two, a young Indian boy appeared from somewhere in the house and stood smiling silently. With a nod of her head the old woman indicated the burro on the street, and the boy instantly ran out and grasped the rope.

"Carlos will watch your burro," said the old woman. "Come this way and wait in the patio. Father Hidalgo will see you. He sees everyone."

As he followed her through a narrow entrance-way, Nando had a brief glimpse into a cool, dark room on either side. They were not luxuriously furnished, certainly nothing to compare with the Rodriguez household, or even with the rooms in his own hacienda, but Nando sensed that the *cura* of this poor little parish lived comfortably.

The servant led him into a central patio, which the afternoon sun filled with light and shadows, and told him to wait. Then she disappeared through one of the doors, and Nando was left alone.

It was not a beautiful patio, for no one had bothered to plant flowers. In some of the rough squares which formed the floor, spaces had been left for a few trees, and one of these was covered with small oranges, the kind that pucker the mouth. The other trees were without fruit. There was a well in the middle, with an arched top from which hung a bucket, and the white plaster figure of the Virgin stood guard on an adjoining ledge.

The house itself was a square, running around all four sides of the center patio. The street walls served also as outer walls for the living quarters, and because they were thick and deep the rooms were cool and refreshing on the hottest day. An arched porch ran around the interior walls overlooking the patio, the roof of which gave protection from the noon sun, and at intervals wooden benches had been placed, an invitation to sit and relax.

From the open door through which the woman had disappeared Nando could now hear the flap, flap, flap of tortillas being molded out by hand. Undoubtedly dinner preparations were underway, and he hoped wistfully that he would be invited to stay. Isobel had not thought to send along a nine o'clock breakfast, and he had not eaten since five.

Five o'clock was a very long time ago, and he had trudged many miles since then. Although the servant had not invited him to do so he sat down on the bricks lining the well, but as a long shadow fell across the sunny courtyard, he jumped to his feet, snatching the sombrero from his head.

A man had come out from one of the doors, a man dressed in dark knee breeches, waistcoat, and jacket made of goods which came to the colonies by ship from India and was called *rompacoche*. He was of medium height, and his shoulders were slightly stooped so that his bald head, with the long fringe of white hair around the sides and back, was inclined forward. He was leaning on a cane as he stood there smiling and regarding Nando with unusually keen gray eyes.

"Yes, my son?" His voice questioned Nando's business with him.

"You are Father Hidalgo," gasped Nando, and through his mind flashed a memory of his reception at the hands of this man's brother. "I bring you a letter, Señor *Cura*. A letter from the Señorita Isobel Rodriguez."

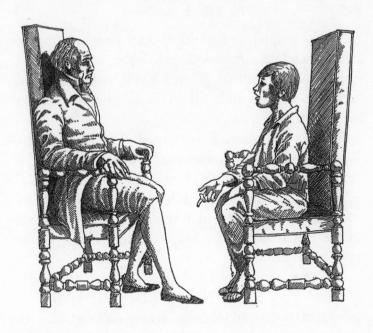

8

"From Señorita Isobel Rodriguez?" repeated Father
Hidalgo, and a twinkle shone in the gray eyes beneath the white brows. "Now what message could
the señorita have for me which is so important that
it cannot wait for my next visit to San Miguel el
Grande?"

He took the now crumpled sheet of paper from
Nando and his mouth quivered, as though it was
only by an effort that he restrained a smile.

"You are to wait for an answer, of course? A
communication of such importance would require an
immediate reply."

Nando gulped and nodded. Any minute now, he told himself, the *cura* will break the seal and read what is written within. Then he will look at me and decide it is a lie and call someone to throw me in the street.

"Let us sit down," suggested Father Hidalgo. "There is a bench in the shade where we can be more comfortable while I am reading my letter."

Silently Nando followed him toward the house, and when the priest had taken his seat the boy sat on the other end of the long wooden bench, as far away as possible.

Almost as soon as he began reading, the smile vanished from Father Hidalgo's face. He looked up once and inspected Nando closely before his eyes returned to the paper. When he had finished, he folded it carefully.

"You are Fernando de Fuentes of Puebla de los Angeles?" His tone was matter of fact and held no apparent doubt.

"Of the Hacienda del Fuentes," corrected Nando. "It's a half day's ride from there. My brother Alejandro lives in Puebla."

"So the Señorita Isobel has informed me. She also says that you have a most fascinating tale to relate of your recent adventures, and that she wishes me to hear it from your own lips. She vouches, however, most earnestly, for your identity. Suppose you tell me exactly what has happened to you."

Nando took a deep breath and began. He found

it quite easy to talk with Father Hidalgo, who listened quietly without interruption, nodding from time to time as a signal that he understood, perhaps even sympathized.

"That Isobel!" he declared when Nando fell silent. "Everything is clear except her own part. Why didn't she tell my brother who you were? Why did she have to drag you out of your way to Dolores under, I am sure, the most uncomfortable conditions to you, so that you could tell your story to me?"

Nando was silent. He couldn't admit to this good man that Isobel had sent him here to act as a spy. At least that had been her plan, although Nando himself intended to have no part in anything so underhanded.

"Perhaps it is her sex which explains her behavior," decided the *cura* after a moment. "I have never pretended to understand women. I only admire their beauty and grace. But Isobel Rodriguez has always seemed to have an unusually sharp mind for one so young. I had thought—but never mind. The problem with which we must concern ourselves is what to do about you."

"Yes, Father," said Nando meekly. Although he had met this man only a few minutes before, he already had the feeling that Father Hidalgo could cope with any problem.

"We must notify your brother Alejandro, first of all." The *cura* looked at Nando sternly. "The poor young man must be nearly out of his mind with worry. I will write a letter tonight. The first traveler bound for Mexico City will carry it to my brother. I will instruct him to forward it to Puebla at the first opportunity."

"Yes, Father," said Nando again. It would take a long time for a letter to reach Alejandro in this manner, but it was of no importance. He couldn't believe that his brother was as worried about him as the *cura* insisted.

"Then we must see about a bath for you." Father Hidalgo's nose wrinkled suggestively and Nando felt overwhelmed by shame. He knew he was very dirty. Perhaps he even smelled offensive. Reading his mind, the *cura* smiled to soften the disgrace and continued counting off items on his long fingers. "After that, dinner. For I am sure you are hungry. Then we must see about some suitable clothes. Meanwhile, we will find something which will do temporarily, but I am afraid they will not suffice for Don Fernando de Fuentes."

Nando smiled. The title sounded good in his ears. He had been afraid that it would never be his again.

"I am to stay here with you?" he asked timidly.

"I can't think of any other place for you to stay," the *cura* told him frankly. "I think it would be advisable until we hear from your brother Don Alejandro. Have you any objections to staying here?"

"Oh no. I'd like it very much," cried Nando eagerly.

He had his bath in the *cura*'s own tub. It was carried into the small bedchamber which had been assigned to him, and Concha, the old woman who had greeted him at the door, also brought clean white cotton garments to replace his dirty rags. They were too large, and doubtless belonged to one of Father Hidalgo's servants, but Nando didn't care.

After Concha had poured hot water into the tin tub and gone away, Nando sat in it and scrubbed himself with soap. Even after he was sure he was clean, he continued to sit there a long time. Hot water, which he had always taken for granted, had become a real luxury.

Later, at the conclusion of their simple meal, Father Hidalgo led Nando into a small room in which were two high-backed chairs with wide seats and carved arms. A candle burned in its holder on the table, and against the wall were two shelves filled with books. The *cura*'s eyes gleamed as he looked at them.

"These are my friends," he said nodding toward the leather-bound volumes. "They bring me great pleasure, and there is one for every mood. If I wish to be merry, there are Molière's comedies to amuse me. If I am sad, Racine's tragedies can match my mood. If I wish to improve my mind there are books filled with knowledge. There are history, theology, drama—which do you prefer?"

"I—I don't know," admitted Nando. He walked

over to one of the cases, and at a nodded permission
from the *cura* he took one of the volumes from the
shelf.

"Why, this is in a strange language," he cried in
amazement. "I can't even read it."

"There are books in Spanish, too." Father Hidalgo
smiled and came to look over his shoulder. "That
one is in French."

"You can read French?" Nando was greatly impressed.

"Also Italian." The *cura* shrugged off the accom-
plishment as though it was of no importance. "And
of course, Latin. That was necessary when I studied
theology at Valladolid. Once I had mastered Latin,
both Italian and French were easy, since they, like
Spanish, are derived from that language. Greek, I
found a little harder. It was a challenge."

"Isobel said you were very wise," remembered
Nando.

"The señorita is kind," said Father Hidalgo. His
face grew thoughtful and a little sad. "The *Inquisición* does not take so flattering a view of my scholas-
tic achievements."

"What do you mean?" Nando's mind returned to
the pile of fagots being laid in the *zócalo* for a
victim of the *Inquisición*'s wrath.

Father Hidalgo noticed the fear on the boy's face
and tried to laugh it away.

"Bless you, my son, didn't you know that there
was a file on me at *Inquisición* headquarters? The

charge is heresy. The grounds are that I read too much, of books which are not on the list approved by the Holy Church. Why, I have even been known to praise some books which have been put on the Index *Expurgatorius!*" He laughed heartily at the last sentence.

"But the *Inquisición*," quavered Nando, "it does terrible things to people. I saw them myself in Mexico City."

The *cura* came over and patted Nando on the shoulder.

"Do not worry," he said. "The charges against me were dropped. My file was closed. It is lucky that I have a brother who is a *licenciado* and a member of the *Inquisición*. Do you not agree? Now, shall I choose you a book? An innocent, harmless, amusing book in Spanish?"

"With your permission, Father," said Nando weakly, "I am very tired. It has been a long day. If I could go to bed—"

"Of course. I am a thoughtless old man." The *cura* sounded distressed that the idea had not occurred to him. "Go to bed, Nando, and God grant you sweet dreams."

He whisked a book from the shelf and had already settled down in one of the chairs close to the candle before Nando could leave the room.

The next day was Sunday. Father Hidalgo said two morning masses, and Nando attended them both because he felt it would be a discourtesy to his host to do otherwise.

There was only one church in Dolores, always referred to as the *parroquia*. Perhaps because it was small, Nando felt more at home within its stone walls than he had in the magnificent cathedral at Puebla. It reminded him a little of the small chapel on the Hacienda del Fuentes.

He still wore the garments of a peon, for it had been impossible to find suitable clothing for a young creole in Dolores. The poor shops of the village did not boast garments so fine. The *cura* had suggested cutting down some of his own woolen garments, but Nando had quickly refused the offer.

"These are fine," he insisted, patting the clean white cotton of his shirt. "Besides, until we hear from Alejandro, and he sends money, I cannot pay."

They walked home together after the last service, carrying on a rather disjointed conversation as they went. The *cura* was constantly being stopped by his parishioners, who wished to inquire about his health and, incidentally, propound some problem which demanded immediate solution. Nando could see by their faces that they loved Father Hidalgo.

"This is not a very rich parish," observed Nando. Even in Sunday best, the clothes of the residents of Dolores were in bad condition.

"Nor will it grow richer," said Father Hidalgo sadly. "Once I had hopes for the village. I opened a factory and imported a workman who was skilled

in making fine china—not the crude pottery turned
out by the people from red clay. He was teaching
them his skill, and they were learning, too—"

He broke off abruptly.

"Good morning, Señora Valdez. I did not see your
husband in mass this morning. I trust he is not
ill."

Nando waited patiently while the señora explained
why it had been impossible for her husband to attend mass. After that he waited while the *cura* inquired into the health of other members of the
Valdez family in turn.

"You were telling me about the pottery," he said,
when once again they were on their way.

"Oh yes. The pottery. As I said, the people were
doing well. It could have been sold and would have
brought in a little revenue. Then I persuaded some
of the farmers to plant grapes. Would you believe
it, there was once a fine vineyard right over there
in that empty field! Wine, you understand. That's
what I had in mind. People pay for wine, alas,
when they will not pay for bread. And mulberry
trees! I bought some young mulberry trees, which
should do well in this climate. Silkworms feed on
them, you know."

Again he broke off for another conversation with
one of his parishioners. Nando could hardly wait
until it was concluded and he could ask the important question.

"What happened to them? To the pottery works, and the vineyard, and the mulberry trees?"

"The soldiers came and did away with them." Father Hidalgo's cane pounded angrily on the cobblestones. "They smashed the potter's wheels. They dug up the vineyards and cut down the mulberry."

"But why?"

"These things, fine pottery and china, wine and silk, are not permitted to be produced in the colonies of Spain," Father Hidalgo told him. "We must buy them, import them by ship, and pay a very high price for them, more than we can afford. So most of us do without."

"That doesn't seem fair," said Nando in surprise.

The Hacienda del Fuentes had been furnished years ago, and the imported needs of Don Anselmo had been few. True, he had complained about the high cost of his own and Nando's clothing, and the tax on snow, which his own peons brought from the mountains for refrigeration, threw him into a rage every time he remembered it, but he had been content to grow maize and raise fine black horses.

"No, it doesn't seem fair that Mexico should be bled to increase the wealth of the viceroy and of Spain," agreed the *cura* softly. "But it has been going on a long time, my son. With Carlos III on the throne we hoped things would improve—and they did, a little. That was when the creoles were permitted to buy commissions in the Army, and to become *licenciados,* and to climb a little higher in church rank. But that was years ago, and there have been no reforms since then. This is 1810, and people argue about who should sit on the throne of Spain, Fernando VII or the brother of the Frenchman, Napoleon Bonaparte. These are difficult times. Difficult times."

"Yes, sir," agreed Nando meekly. He had never thought about such things. On the hacienda they were of little importance.

As they neared his home, Father Hidalgo cried out in delight.

"We have visitors, Nando. Friends. Hurry, we must not keep them waiting."

As soon as he saw the horse at the door, Nando had a premonition of alarm. The horse had a military saddle, the kind that Ramón always used, and it was being held by an Indian in the uniform of an army private. Captain Allende was twenty miles away in San Miguel el Grande, he reminded himself sternly. There was no reason for him to be calling at the house of Father Hidalgo.

But as he followed the *cura* through the entranceway and into the sunny patio he saw that his worst fears were realized. The soldier who was pacing impatiently back and forth between the bitter orange tree and the well, absently striking at his high Spanish boots with his riding crop, was Ramón's friend.

"Don Ignacio," cried the *cura* in a pleased voice, and his cane tapped against the stones as he hurried forward. "A pleasure indeed." His voice took on a sudden anxious quality. "Nothing is wrong?"

"No, nothing at all," Captain Allende assured him quickly. "I only came to inform you of a special meeting of our club in Querétaro on Tuesday night."

"Tuesday? Then we can ride there together," decided Father Hidalgo promptly. "If you will accept my hospitality tonight, we can set out tomorrow early."

"Exactly what I had in mind," approved the soldier. "There is new information. Someone has just returned from the City of Mexico—" He broke off suddenly, his eyes falling on Nando, who had stopped self-consciously at the doorway.

"You must meet my guest," said Father Hidalgo promptly, his eyes following the captain's. He turned and beckoned the boy forward. "Captain Ignacio Allende, permit me to introduce Don Fernando de Fuentes."

Allende took a step forward. On his face was an expression of great disbelief. He blinked his eyes and stared hard at the short, square figure in the white cotton garments of a peon.

"Nando?" he said after a moment. "Nando, is it you?"

"You know each other?" Father Hidalgo was delighted. "Why, this is a wonderful thing."

"Nando, what are you doing here? And dressed in this manner?" Don Ignacio's voice was sharp with disapproval, but Nando gave a happy sigh of relief.

In just such severe tones, underlaid with deep affection, would Ramón have spoken had he been standing there in place of his friend. Captain Allende was not going to turn away! He had not changed!

Nando forgot that he was a great boy of thirteen years. He ran to his friend, clasping the captain about his waist, burying his face in the immaculate blue and white uniform. The officer patted him on the shoulder, and Nando could hear his voice explaining their relationship to the *cura*.

"His brother is one of my best friends. I have visited with Ramón often on the Hacienda del Fuentes. Why, together we taught Nando the *coleada* of the bulls. It is incredible to find him here like this. Does Ramón know?"

"I am sure he doesn't," said Father Hidalgo dryly. "It is a long story, which Nando shall tell you himself. I am writing to his brother Alejandro at Puebla. It seems that no one knew where to find the other brother."

"He is at San Luis Potosí. He is with General Calleja," said Allende. Nando wondered if he was mistaken in detecting a slight edge in his voice. "Ramón de Fuentes is a fine soldier. A loyal subject of his majesty, the king."

"Commendable. Commendable," declared the *cura*. "Now, Nando, if you will loose your hold, suppose we all sit down so you can repeat your story for Don Ignacio's benefit."

Once again Nando went through the account of

his adventures, but unlike Father Hidalgo, Allende was not a silent listener. He deplored the tragic death of Don Anselmo and promised to have a mass said for his soul. With many apologies to Father Hidalgo, he condemned Alejandro's decision to make a priest of Nando. Anyone who rode so well, who faced the bulls so bravely in the *coleada*, would find his talents wasted in anything but the military. Unless, of course, Nando preferred to run the hacienda. That was a fine pursuit for a gentleman also. He cursed the bandits who had stolen the boy's clothes and horse, and it was with a visible effort that he restrained himself from commenting on the behavior of the *licenciado*. Like the *cura* he was most amazed at Isobel Rodriguez for bringing Nando to Dolores.

"That girl!" He shook his long, handsome head with its fine crest of wavy, brown hair. "I have never met one like her before, and the good God grant that I never do again. So full of questions on every subject! So curious about matters which are of no concern to ladies! And the imagination which she possesses you would not believe possible. I would worry if I were her father."

"I think he does a little," admitted Father Hidalgo thoughtfully. "But what can he do?"

"There are ways," insisted Captain Allende darkly.

"She is the only child left to them," remembered Father Hidalgo. "Six children were born to Doña

Triumfa. The angels took five when they were mere infants."

"All the more reason why the one remaining should be a credit to her parents," concluded Allende. He turned and regarded Nando thoughtfully. "I agree with the *cura* that you must stay here with him until we hear from your brothers. But we must do something about your clothes."

"Exactly what I've been thinking." Father Hidalgo leaned forward earnestly. "It is a problem. Here in Dolores, where I have credit, there are no shops which sell suitable clothing. But if you could vouch for the bill in San Miguel el Grande, I would pay you back."

"No need. I will pay for them myself," promised Allende. He grew thoughtful. "There are shops in San Miguel, of course. But there is a better tailor in Querétaro. Why don't we take Nando with us when we leave tomorrow for the meeting?"

"Splendid," agreed the *cura* instantly, but Nando felt a sense of uneasiness.

This club meeting was undoubtedly the one about which Isobel Rodriguez was so curious. He resolved to close his ears to any scraps of information which might fall his way. He didn't trust Isobel. She would wangle anything he heard out of him before he knew it.

9

The last time he had been in Querétaro he had
been riding on the Rodriguez coach step, and in
his tired, bruised condition Nando had found no
time to study the town. On this visit he had opportunity to inspect it more thoroughly from the back
of a mule. Father Hidalgo had only one horse, and
naturally it was proper that he ride that himself.

Querétaro was a sleepy town where grass grew in
the middle of the streets and at every corner was
a small open square filled with trees. A great aque-
duct, built on stone arches, brought water from the
mountains five miles away so that the palms and

banana trees bending over the walks looked fresh and green, and the roses and poppies, geraniums and lilies grew tall and luxurious.

To Nando's surprise, they again stayed at the house of the *Corregidor* Miguel Dominguez and his wife, Doña Josefa. And to his even greater amazement, a coach containing Isobel's father, Don Serapio Rodriguez, rolled up soon after they arrived.

Don Serapio was alone. Neither Doña Triumfa nor Isobel accompanied him. Remembering the girl's candid remark that Don Serapio's attendance of these literary meetings was only an excuse to get away from his wife, Nando smothered a grin.

It was quite an exalted assemblage gathered to discuss books. There were three *licenciados,* including a particular friend of Allende's from San Miguel el Grande named Ignacio Aldama, four army officers, the *alcalde* of Querétaro, the *corregidor,* and several others of equal importance. All were creoles, and when Father Hidalgo and Captain Allende vouched for Nando they accepted him as one, too.

He was more than a little amazed when Don Serapio did not recognize him, but perhaps it was only natural. There was small resemblance between the ragged, dirty boy who had clung to the Rodriguez coach step and the clean lad attired in the new silks purchased by Captain Allende in one of the shops.

Nando was not invited to attend the meeting. He noticed that Father Hidalgo had a book under his arm when he left to go upstairs with the others and he concluded that their literary discussions would center on that. It was in French, and Nando thought that it was no wonder Don Serapio went to sleep during the evenings.

The meeting lasted well into the night. Nando was only dimly aware of Captain Allende, with whom he shared a room, coming to bed. The long session must have left everyone feeling very tired, for as they broke up to say good-by the next morning there were few smiles, only long, serious faces.

The return ride to San Miguel el Grande was begun in silence. Nando would have liked to speak, but the stern, set faces of the other two kept his lips closed.

"It is intolerable!" declared Allende, finally breaking the long quiet. "Francisco Venegas is a soldier, and an unsuccessful general at that! What does he know of the needs of the colonies? He has never even been here before. He sees us as an opportunity to fill his own coffers, as he was unable to do in the war against the English."

"Hush," cautioned Father Hidalgo hastily, with a quick glance at Nando.

Now that he had started, Allende was not to be silenced.

"And new taxes," he stormed. "Now they amount to sixty percent of everything we own. Why the treasure ship which sails from Mexico to Spain next February will sink from the weight of our gold."

"Don Ignacio, I beg of you," pleaded Father Hidalgo in alarm.

"Oh, Nando's used to hearing people complain about taxes. He knows it means nothing." But Captain Allende looked a little shamefaced. "I've heard his father on the subject of taxes, and so has he."

"Of a certainty," agreed Nando promptly, anxious to put the older man at ease. "Alejandro, too, complains about the taxes he must pay."

"And Ramón?" asked the *cura* quickly.

Nando shook his head. He had never heard Ramón mention taxes. Perhaps they did not occur to him.

They would spend the night at San Miguel el Grande, Father Hidalgo announced. He was weary, too tired for the remaining twenty miles to Dolores. Allende immediately asked them both to stay at his house, but the *cura* smilingly declined.

"Don Serapio extended an invitation last night and I accepted. Besides," with a teasing glance at the boy on the mule, "it will give Nando a chance to visit with his benefactress, the Señorita Isobel."

Nando's heart sank. He had no wish to see Isobel Rodriguez again. She was sure to ply him with questions the moment she managed to get him alone. But at least, he thought gleefully, she will find out nothing, for I know nothing.

The Rodriguez family greeted them warmly. Like her husband, Doña Triumfa did not recognize Nando, and Isobel gave no sign that she had ever seen him before. She curtsied deeply and murmured that it gave her great pleasure to meet any friend of the *cura's*.

"Perhaps, Mama," she suggested, "you would like me to show Fernando the patio? I am sure he does not enjoy sitting quietly on a stiff chair while his elders talk, any more than I do."

"Isobel!" Doña Triumfa smiled a weak apology for her daughter's rudeness toward Father Hidalgo.

"At least she speaks frankly," said the *cura*. "Perhaps the two children can find something to discuss between them. Why not give your permission, Doña Triumfa?"

Put that way, the lady had no choice but to give in, and Nando glumly followed the victorious Isobel through the house to the central patio.

"Now, tell me everything," she ordered, settling herself on a bench in the shade of a bougainvillea vine. "You went with them to Querétaro, I know. Papa told us. Did you get to attend their precious literary society meeting?"

"No."

"Didn't you even get an idea what it was about? Didn't someone say something?"

"Not a single word. But I'm sure they discussed a book. Father Hidalgo had one under his arm."

"What was the name of it? What was it about?" She pounced on the small fragment eagerly.

"How should I know." Nando grinned at her. "It was written in French."

To his surprise she considered the statement carefully.

"French! There are a lot of French here in Mexico. They're not thought well of at all. People say they are heretics. But I suppose that will change if Joseph Napoleon manages to hold the throne."

Here was Nando's chance to go into the matter of the succession of the throne of Spain, a subject which Father Hidalgo had introduced on Sunday and about which the boy had known nothing. He had wondered about it since, but was too shy to confess his ignorance to the *cura*. He didn't mind asking Isobel. Since he didn't like her anyway, he didn't care what she thought of him.

"I wish you'd tell me about that," he admitted. "What has Napoleon got to do with our king?"

"Oh, you poor innocent from the distant provinces," Isobel sighed with elaborate mock pity. "You just don't know anything about anything, do you? But it's a real intrigue. It's far deeper than any little scheme dreamed up by a silly old literary society in Querétaro."

"Are you going to tell me or not?" asked Nando stiffly.

"Certainly." Isobel's eyes sparkled, and she began at once. "Well, the last good king of Spain was Carlos III, I suppose you know about him. Captain Allende or any other creole wouldn't have been allowed to be an officer in the Army if it hadn't been for Carlos III." She broke off to look at Nando sharply. "How did you get so friendly with Captain Allende so soon?"

"I knew him before," Nando told her shortly. "He's a friend of my brothers."

"Oh." Isobel considered this for a moment before she continued. "Well, Carlos III passed good laws, but then he died and we had Carlos IV. He didn't do anything for Mexico and not much for Spain either. He must not have liked being king because he abdicated in favor of his son Fernando. About that time Napoleon Bonaparte marched into Madrid with a big army. He made Fernando renounce the throne and named his own brother, Joseph Bonaparte, king of Spain."

"Why that's terrible," cried Nando. He wondered if Father Hidalgo knew about this dreadful situation. He might not enjoy reading French literature so much if he did.

"Isn't it an intrigue?" beamed Isobel happily. "Then Napoleon invited Fernando to come to France, and when the stupid man arrived he was thrown into a dungeon. That's where he is now. Everybody takes sides, naturally. Most of the creoles in Mexico side with Fernando, and the *gachupines* favor Bonaparte."

"Why?" gasped Nando. "He isn't even a Spaniard!"

"Oh, they have to take sides. They always do on everything," explained Isobel airily. "But there are more creoles here in Mexico than *gachupines*, so Fernando is the favorite."

"It can't do him much good if he's stuck away in a dungeon."

"Oh, but it does," she assured him triumphantly. "You see, Spain wants us to send men to help them fight their old wars in Europe. They're always having a war with somebody. And the creoles won't go. The viceroy José Iturrigary tried to make them, so somebody kidnapped him and packed him off by ship to Spain. Then we appointed our own viceroys here in Mexico." She paused to frown thoughtfully to herself. "The trouble was, the first one they picked was too old. His name was de Garibay, and he used to be commander in chief of the army. But he was over 80 years old and they needed somebody younger. So they chose the Archbishop of Mexico, Francisco de Lizana y Beaumont. They were both *gachupines*, and they had been appointed by the king to their first jobs, so you'd think they would have been acceptable—"

"But they weren't, because Spain is sending us a new viceroy," interrupted Nando remembering Allende's explosive remarks on the way from Querétaro. "A general!"

"How did you know?" Isobel demanded quickly, her eyes narrowing. "I thought nobody knew. Papa heard about it in Mexico City. I heard him tell Mama. Of course, they thought it wasn't important, but I wondered at the time if it wasn't a new intrigue. How did you know about the new viceroy?"

"I guess I overheard your father telling someone in Querétaro," said Nando uncomfortably.

"Oh." Isobel sounded disappointed. "Papa! I thought it might be something important, but if it was just Papa—"

"I heard somebody complaining about taxes, too," suggested Nando cautiously.

Isobel made a little face.

"That doesn't mean a thing. They're always crying about that. What I'm looking for is a real intrigue. Something mysterious and secret. I'll have to think about that French book, although it may not amount to much. You keep listening and remember everything you hear so you can tell me."

The June rains began the day after they reached Dolores. Father Hidalgo wrote the letter to Alejandro, but by now few travelers were venturing so far as Mexico City on slippery mud roads. It was a long time before it was started on its way.

Rain and muddy roads were not enough to discourage shorter trips, however. Captain Allende rode over at least twice a month from San Miguel el Grande, and Father Hidalgo made a trip to Querétaro whenever the literary society held a meeting. Nando was never asked to accompany him again. He was told to stay at home with his books, for the *cura* had insisted that the boy resume his studies.

Father Hidalgo was an exacting teacher, much more so than any of the tutors on the hacienda.

But his warm smile of approval when Nando had done well was worth working for, so the boy studied hard.

The summer raced by on hot, moist feet and Nando began to regain some of the security which had been his on the Hacienda del Fuentes. Only it wasn't quite the same.

It had not occurred to Captain Allende to buy more than one suit of silk clothes appropriate for a creole. On the morning of the purchase he had been rather distracted, as though his mind was busy with more important matters, and Nando hadn't liked to call it to his attention. Since there was as yet no word from Alejandro, Nando decided it was prudent to save his good clothes for Sunday and special occasions. On weekdays when he was studying or walking around the village, he put on the white cotton garments which Concha had found for him on the day of his arrival.

The strange thing was that each change of clothing seemed to bring a change of personality. In silk, he was the young creole, inclined to summon an Indian to bring him a drink of water or to light the candle at twilight. In the cotton shirt and breeches of a peon, he invariably fetched his own water, lighted his own candle, and ran his own errands. And the way he was treated by the people of Dolores fit into the same pattern. They smiled and joked with the boy in peon clothes, making him feel that he was their friend. But when they saw the silken suit approaching they stepped into the street, returning his greeting civilly but refusing to meet his eye.

Concha, with whom he tried to discuss this strange state of affairs, had a very unsatisfactory answer.

"The *gachupines* are all bad," she declared. "They are evil men who think the Indian is less than their own horses."

"But I'm not *gachupín*," he insisted. "I'm a creole."

"They are both white," she reminded him, and Nando, who had begun the conversation after mass, dressed in his fine clothes, wished he had done so on a weekday.

Father Hidalgo's explanation was more logical, but it left Nando feeling a little uneasy.

"Have you a good friend who is a *gachupín*, Nando?"

"The *gachupines* are friends only to each other," Nando reminded him quickly. "They think, because they were born in Spain, that they are better than us. Do you know what they say, Father? They say it is the climate of Mexico which gets into the blood and makes the creoles inferior! They say the poor blood addles our brains, and that is why we cannot hold responsible positions. I do not like the *gachupines*. I spit on them," he finished with an appropriate gesture.

"And have you a good friend who is an Indian?"

"Of course." Nando's thoughts turned immediately to Cardito. "One who is a faithful, loyal servant."

"But still a servant?" asked Father Hidalgo quickly.

"He is only an Indian."

"He is a servant because his skin is not the color of ours." The *cura* shook his head sadly. "We look down on the Indians for the color of their skins, and they resent us and the *gachupines* for the color of ours. They link us together because of that. But the real reason for their resentment is our treatment of them for the last three hundred years."

"On the Hacienda del Fuentes we treat our *Inditos* kindly. We look after them and protect them. That's why they stay with us," Nando explained.

"Is it?" The brilliant gray eyes looked searchingly into his. "On the hacienda your peons are paid wages?"

"Of course."

"Isn't it true that almost every peon has borrowed against his wages?"

"They are permitted to do that, yes." For some reason Nando was beginning to feel a little uncomfortable.

"They are not permitted to leave the service of their *patrón* until the debt is paid in full?"

"A man must pay what he owes," said Nando stiffly.

"Ay, and he must pay the debts of his father as

well," agreed the *cura*. "A peon inherits his father's debt, along with any worldly goods he owns. You say that your workers stay with you because they love you. Is it not because they will never be out of debt, and so they cannot leave?"

Nando looked away. Although he had never thought of it before, what the *cura* had said was very true.

With September, the rains began to lessen. The brown flats about Dolores had changed to soft green, and the bedraggled trees in Father Hidalgo's patio lifted their branches with new life. The mountains to the north, which climbed upward to Guanajuato, the city of mines, sparkled in the rain-washed air, and seemed much nearer at hand than in the arid months of winter.

On the evening of the fifteenth, Nando had gone to bed later than usual. He had been working over a page of Latin, more difficult than any he had encountered before, and he was determined to conquer it. The house was very still. The servants had retired long ago, and Father Hidalgo had finally gone to his room. The sleeping quarters were on the side street, and a ray of moonlight slipped through the iron bars across the high window to fall on Nando's cot. In spite of the hour he was wide awake, and through eyes which stubbornly refused to close he watched the streak of light.

Suddenly he sat up in bed. The open window admitted other things besides moonlight. He could hear the sound of horses' hooves beating against the cobblestones of the street. Two, no three horsemen were advancing at a fast gallop, rousing the good people of Dolores from their well-earned slumbers.

The hoofbeats kept coming nearer, then stopped. A minute later the strident voice of the gate bell clanged its announcement that someone without desired to be admitted.

Nando was out of bed in an instant. In the moonlight he began putting on the clothes he had just discarded, the white cotton garments of a peon. It took him a few seconds, and in that short time Father Hidalgo was before him. As Concha came yawning and complaining from her doorway and Nando stepped out of his, the *cura,* in his long white nightdress and lace-trimmed cap, was opening the outer gate.

Three men stepped quickly inside. They were booted and spurred for riding, and their faces were tense. Nando recognized them all, the three Ignacios: Perez, the *alcalde* of Querétaro; Aldama, the *licenciado* from San Miguel el Grande; and Allende, the soldier and friend of his brother Ramón.

"Father, we are found out!" cried *Alcalde* Perez dramatically.

"The time is here before we are prepared," added *Licenciado* Aldama.

"I'm afraid we're caught in a trap. There's no way out but to spring it," concluded Captain Allende.

"If what you imply is correct, the situation calls

for action," said Father Hidalgo severely. "We have no other course but to go out and seize the *gachupines* tonight."

Nando stared with open mouth. So Isobel had been right after all. There had been intrigue brewing under the guise of a harmless literary society.

10

"Summon everyone in the household." Father Hidalgo turned to speak over his shoulder to the open-mouthed Concha. "See that you forget no one, particularly the able-bodied men. Every one will count."

With a hasty apology to the three visitors he made his way back to his own room to dress in more suitable clothing.

Nando stood where he was, wondering what was expected of him. As a member of the household he was included in the *cura*'s proposed meeting, but meanwhile he felt a little stupid doing nothing. He would have liked to cross over to the creoles, who were plainly visible in the light of the full moon, but their faces were so stern that he was afraid he would not be welcome.

"You're certain that you and the Doña Josefa did not jump to conclusions?" Captain Allende spoke to the *Alcalde* Perez, but his voice carried quite plainly to where Nando was standing.

"There can be no mistake," insisted Perez firmly. "One of our group was very ill. He was sure he was dying, otherwise he would never have made his confession to the priest. Alas, he told everything. He implicated not only himself but the rest of us who have been gathering regularly for the meetings. Later, when he began to recover his health, he admitted the whole thing to me. He was beginning to have reservations about the priest—a certain coolness, you understand. We were afraid—the *corregidor*, Doña Josefa, and I, that the priest would break his seal of silence and inform the authorities. That is why we conceived this little signal between us, in case they came. Whoever was taken first was pledged to knock on the floor three times, and the other was to spread the alarm."

"So when the soldiers came to the house and he heard the knocking on the floor, the *alcalde* rode to San Miguel el Grande," interrupted Aldama. "We sent out word immediately, so that our friends there could take cover. Then the two of us followed you here."

"A pity that I came here today with so small a detachment," frowned Captain Allende. "I'm not too sure of the regular garrison stationed in Dolores. But my own command will follow me to a man."

"I feel that all members of the club should collect in one place," declared Aldama. "If we must make a stand, let us do it together."

"Very heroic," Captain Allende's voice sounded a little dry. "In one place, we can all be taken together. I, for one, prefer a little better odds."

In answer to Concha's summons, the servants were beginning to gather in the moonlight, the gardeners, the man who swept the street before the house, the *criadas*, the stablemen, the cook and her assistants, the laundress, as well as those who worked in the *parroquia*, the two bell ringers, the sacristan, the cleaners, and the grave diggers from the cemetery. In all, there were thirty persons collected in the patio when Father Hidalgo, wearing a long, dark, woolen cloak over his usual ecclesiastical garments, came from his room. Leaning on his cane he made his way to the well, where he took up a stand beside the statue of the Virgin.

"My children, this is a momentous night." He began speaking immediately in the loud, ringing tones with which he addressed his parishioners at mass. "You, of Dolores, are entitled to know what has happened. Before long all of Mexico must know. We did not think to tell you so soon. We had planned to proclaim ourselves next December, at the great fair at San Juan de los Lagos. But our plans have been found out. We have no choice but to announce them now, before our preparations are complete.

"For the last few years a handful of us have been meeting to discuss the sorry condition of his majesty's subjects who reside in Mexico. Not the newly arrived, the *gachupines,* but those of us who are born here."

There was a low muttering among the now wide-awake Indians as he said the word *gachupín.* Father Hidalgo lifted a warning hand and silenced the murmuring.

"We feel that the time has come to demand certain reforms. We have had enough of viceroys and archbishops from Spain who know nothing of the needs of our country. We abhor the heavy taxes which pour into the royal coffers and leave us hungry. We resent that we are prevented from starting any industry of our own, but must purchase all our goods from Spain. We, in this colony, are capable of bettering our condition, of creating a richer life for ourselves and our families. But this right is denied us by royal command. Did not the soldiers cut your grape vines and smash your potter's wheels because wine and fine dishes are made in Spain and we must buy what they make? Apart from the precious metals dug from Mexican earth, all we are permitted to export are cochineal and indigo. That is not right. It should not be.

"The men who gathered behind closed doors are

not revolutionists in that we deny our king certain rights. But we feel that we, too, have rights. We feel that the rights of Mexico, and of any colony of Spain, must be respected. Will you help us make a stand? Will you march and fight, perhaps even die, to help secure your rights? Your independence?"

With the others Nando stood entranced as he listened to the *cura*. The timber of his voice was even more moving than the words. The moonlight turned the fringe of white hair to silver, and it glistened about his high domed head like the halo of a saint. His brilliant eyes flashed with compelling vigor, and Nando heard his own voice chiming in with those of the servants.

"Lead, Father! We will follow."

Father Hidalgo smiled. He beckoned to the three creoles, and as they left the patio the men of his household fell in behind. Nando went, too, his heart thumping with such excitement that it sounded like a drumbeat in his ears.

In the moonlight the little company made its way to the *parroquia* of Dolores, and at a signal from the *cura*, the bell ringers sprang forward to the ropes. In the clear September air, the clapper pounded savagely against the iron sides of the bell. A dozen times it rang before Father Hidalgo held up his hand for silence.

The residents of Dolores roused themselves and listened, bleary-eyed. When the tolling ceased, they turned over and went back to sleep, for it was scarcely past midnight. But everyone knew that the ringing of the bell had been a message. Absences would not be tolerated at early mass next morning.

"Now to the public prison," said the *cura* quietly, and his followers turned obediently and started down the cobblestones.

Nando had a moment of uneasiness as he followed. Why should Father Hidalgo want to go to the prison? Prison was where the authorities wished to send him and the others who had been plotting revolt. Surely he wasn't going to give himself up!

When they arrived at the low stone building with its iron-bound door he could see that exactly the reverse was true. Captain Allende drew his sword and demanded the keys from the trembling jailor. Then the prisoners were released, the situation was explained to them, and freedom offered to any who would join the movement. Not a man returned to his cell.

"The *gachupines!* The *gachupines!*" cried one of the new recruits. "Don Fernando Castillo and Don Martin Calderón! Let us take them now and give them a taste of the hard stone cells to which they condemned us."

"In due time," Father Hidalgo told them soothingly. "To gain entrance to the guarded household of a *gachupín* we must have soldiers."

"My detachment at the garrison is loyal," said Captain Allende stoutly. "You can count on them."

It was as he said. The small detachment which

had accompanied him to Dolores that morning responded without question. They left the regular garrison slumbering peacefully and carried out the orders of their captain.

By five o'clock the work was finished. The two Spaniards and certain others who had publicly declared their allegiance to the mother country were occupying the empty spaces in the public prison. Father Hidalgo had sent several of his servants to round up all the available weapons in the village, and others to knock on doors to make sure that no one overslept and missed the early mass. They gathered now in the early light of dawn before the doors of the *parroquia,* for so many had responded to the summons that the small church would not hold them all.

"We will hold mass outside," decided Father Hidalgo, his gray eyes running with approval over the assemblage. "That comes first, for this is the Sabbath, the chosen day of Our Lord. After that I will explain why I have called you together."

Nando obediently fell to his knees on the cobblestones with the others. He had become separated from the members of Father Hidalgo's household, and he was surrounded by a group of villagers. Today, because he was wearing the clothes of a peon, they accepted him. One or two even whispered curious questions about this most unusual behavior of the *cura.* But Nando only shook his head. Father Hidalgo would tell them in his own time.

And tell them he did. His speech, concluding mass, was longer and more impassioned than the brief words he had spent on his own household. His language was simple, his illustrations those which they could understand. He drew a vivid picture of the evils of the government under which they suffered, and in glowing tones held out the advantages which would be theirs with independence.

When he had finished, their shouts rang through the streets of Dolores. *"Viva la Independencia! Viva América!"* and then *"Muerte al mal gobierno!"* Death to bad government!

Since his own servants had not been able to secure weapons for so large a crowd, Father Hidalgo told each man to go home and return with whatever he could find. Unfortunately for Nando, the servants had already stripped the house. All he could produce was a stout stick, a poor weapon for a creole, he told himself angrily. Concha, however, thought even a stick was too much.

"The *cura* does not expect you to go," she told him crossly. "He is too busy to think of you today, or he would tell you so himself. A thirteen-year-old does not fight with the army."

Nando glared at her without answering. If he said too much Concha would capture a minute of the *cura*'s busy time, and then Nando would be told to stay behind. He had no intention of letting that happen. He threw down the stick, letting her think what she pleased, but his mind was made up. He was going.

At eleven o'clock, the motley group reassembled at the *parroquia*. Nando found it easy enough to hide in the crowd, for there were six hundred of them. Outside of a handful of creoles, they were peons, and the weapons they had procured were lances, machetes, and pikes. Only Captain Allende's soldiers were armed with regulation weapons.

The women of Dolores came to say good-by to their men, and Nando tried to secrete himself within the military lines of the untrained peons, which Captain Allende did his best to assemble. It was a fruitless gesture, for as soon as the captain rode back to take his place beside Father Hidalgo in the lead, the men broke ranks. They preferred to advance in a crowd, friends walking and talking together, and stepping on the heels of those before them. Nando pulled his sombrero low on his forehead, crowding on with the others. Fortunately he was able to escape Concha's tearful eyes, and so got out of town.

Before the first hour had passed he began to grow tired. He had been up all night, but excitement had kept the need for sleep from his mind. Now it grew increasingly harder to keep going. The ground seemed to pull at his feet, holding them back, and his eyes stung and burned. But somehow he kept plodding ahead, swept on by the crowd around him. When, after a couple of hours, the leaders halted for a brief rest, Nando slumped to the ground where he stood. He was asleep at once and did not even stir when one of the men good-naturedly tilted his sombrero to shade his face.

After that there was a short rest at the end of each hour's march, and brief as they were they were enough to keep the boy going. The last one was at Atotonilco, the sanctuary which Jesús Ferías, the garrulous soldier, had pointed out the day they traveled the dusty miles to Dolores.

When he saw the two towers with the great tiled dome between, Nando realized they had almost reached their destination. This time he did not sleep. He only lay on the sun-dried earth, hard pounded by the feet of thousands of pilgrims, and rested.

Father Hidalgo dismounted from his horse and climbed the short flight of stairs which led to the massive doors. When he disappeared within, his followers murmured approvingly to each other.

"The good father pauses to ask the blessings of Our Lady upon our cause."

But Father Hidalgo did even more than that. When he returned he carried in his hand the church banner with the picture of the Virgin of Guadalupe.

"My children, here is the symbol of our cause," he cried in ringing tones. "Our Lady of Guadalupe shall lead us in our fight for freedom and independence."

Six hundred hands traced the cross in the warm

air of Atotonilco, and someone improvised a new battle cry which was instantly taken up by the others.

"*Viva Nuestra Señora de Guadalupe! Muerte al mal gobierno!*" Life to Our Lady of Guadalupe. Death to bad government.

Smiling his approval, Father Hidalgo beckoned to one of Allende's soldiers, and when the man reached his side, the *cura* fastened the banner to the soldier's long pike.

"March in front, my son," he ordered. "Our Lady shall lead us from this day on."

Bearing his pike proudly, the man took the lead at the head of the rabble army, and singing and shouting they started on to San Miguel el Grande.

Refreshed by the brief rest stops and buoyed up by excitement, Nando was able to keep up with the others. As they reached the outskirts of town, their numbers were swollen by some of its residents who ran alongside, inquiring the meaning of the invasion. When they understood that it was a concentrated effort to overthrow the suppression of the Spaniards, they pledged their support and joined in. Their numbers crowded the narrow, winding streets, filling them completely from wall to wall, until the horde began to spew out upon the central square.

As soon as they had reached the outskirts of town, Captain Allende's detachment had hurried ahead. He had promised that his whole company would join in the fight for freedom, and he was anxious to gather them under his command. It left only three creoles on horseback, Father Hidalgo, the *Licenciado* Aldama, and the *Alcalde* Perez, at the head of a great host of Indians and *mestizos*. To Nando's alarm he soon realized that the battle cry had now undergone another change.

"*Viva la Virgen de Guadalupe! Muerte a los gachupines!*" shouted the aroused men milling around beneath the leafy trees which overhung the square. Life to the Virgin of Guadalupe! Kill the *gachupines!*

"To the house of the Conde de la Canal!" cried someone. "Let us tear his fine mansion to the ground, stone by stone."

"The brothers Levante!" shouted another. "Don Manuel and Don Victorino. Let us begin with them."

"The *Alcalde* Rodriguez first! His house is just across the square!"

"No, no," shrieked Nando wildly. "There is a difference. A creole is not a *gachupín!* Stop! You are making a mistake."

Father Hidalgo and the two mounted creoles were also alarmed. Their horses reared in protest, but outside of those close by, the crowd was unheeding. Groups started out in every direction toward the great houses close to the square, the house of de Canal, of Lámbarri, of Santoo, of de Loja. Forgotten was the fact that these were families which had lived for years in San Miguel el Grande, that their *gachupín* founder was long entombed in the graveyard close by town, and that his creole descendants suffered under the Spanish king almost as bitterly as the clamoring peons on the square. *Gachupines* were white; creoles were white. In the fired brain of the revolutionists they had become one and the same.

Nando began pushing and squirming through the crowd. His sombrero was knocked from his head, but it didn't matter. With his dark skin and white cotton clothes he looked like all the others. No one paid any attention to his protests, but he kept shouting anyway.

"They are creole, not *gachupines*. They are your allies. They fight for you. The *alcalde* was of the group who started the revolt."

Pushed this way and that he could not be sure that he was even staying in the right direction. He could only try. Isobel Rodriguez was a girl, a helpless, weak girl. As a creole gentleman it was Nando's duty to protect her and her plump, bewildered little parents. He continued on blindly, ducking under arms, jabbing sweaty backs with his elbows until their owners gave way, and at last he saw above him the carvings of two cherubs which ornamented the entrance to the house of Rodriguez.

Someone had already broken down the door, and Nando was part of the crowd which swarmed inside. Through the narrow entranceway they poured,

into the formal salon where Doña Triumfa had received him and Father Hidalgo that night they returned from Querétaro. Chairs were overturned, a
smashed vase which had held roses lay upon the
floor, and as Nando stared in horror one of the
peons pushed out of the crowd and darted across the
room. A moment later he held up a carved ivory
fan which had fallen behind an upended settee.
Nando remembered having seen Doña Triumfa un-
furl it to fan herself, and he wanted to demand that
the man return it immediately. But there was no
time. He was being swept on through the other
rooms, each one of which had been ransacked for
loose trifles and treasure which could be carried
away.

There were three floors to the house of the *alcalde,* and the crowd crept like a swarm of army
ants through every room. In each one Nando expected to find the owner and his family, cowering
before the insults of the invaders, but there was no
trace of any of them. As they started back down the
last flight of stairs, there came the sound of musket
fire outside. The peons stopped short, listening, and
a moment later a voice came floating up from below.

"By order of Father Hidalgo, this looting is to
cease. All loyal Mexicans who follow the banner of
Our Lady will proceed at once to the public
square!"

Instantly subdued and a little shamefaced, the
men continued meekly down the stairs. The voice

had contained a note of authority, and generations
of servitude had trained them to obey without question.

Only Nando stayed where he was. He clung to
the banister, resisting the efforts of those behind
to push him on, so that finally they slipped around
and left him there. When they were gone, when the
house was empty, he sat down on the steps and
put his head in his arms.

Poor Isobel! She had many qualities which he
didn't like, but he hated to think of what must have
happened to her.

11

"Fernando! Fernando de Fuentes!"

Nando came to with a start. Someone was shaking him by the shoulder and speaking his name in a low, urgent voice.

He was still sitting on the stairs which led to the third floor of the Rodriguez house in San Miguel el Grande. He must have fallen asleep after he sat down to mourn the fate of Isobel, for now the stairway was dark with night, and whoever had awakened him was holding a lighted candle in his hand.

"It is the *alcalde*," came the reassuring whisper behind the tiny flare. "The *Alcalde* Serapio Rodriguez. I am on my way to the *mirador*, the looking out place, to see what is going on in the town."

"Don Serapio!" cried Nando happily, scrambling to his feet. "I was afraid you were dead."

The *alcalde* chuckled softly at the idea.

"No." He reassumed his dignity a moment later. "Only feeling a little closed in from the stuffiness of the tunnel which runs underground beneath my house and that of the Conde de la Canal. That is why I volunteered to have a look around. Would you like to come with me? Masquerading in those clothes, I am sure you are perfectly safe."

"Oh yes, señor. Thank you." Nando followed him quickly, for the *alcalde* had taken his acceptance for granted and had not even waited.

Every great house had its *mirador*, a secluded spot on the flat roof which provided a view of the streets below and a portion of the town itself. There were seats on the *mirador* but Don Serapio did not sit down. Instead he placed his elbows on the wide, protecting ledge which extended waist high above the roof and leaned over.

"They are sleeping in the square, and every inch is taken up!" His voice did not suggest resentment of those who had recently broken down his front door and looted his house. Instead he seemed pleased at the magnitude of the crowd.

"There were over six hundred who left Dolores," Nando told him, wonderingly. "And I think that number was doubled when we got here."

"Tripled more likely," corrected the *alcalde* cheerfully. "Dolores is a small town. San Miguel is much bigger. Well, shall we return?"

"Return where?"

"To the tunnel. It is quite comfortable, really, although you will never hear Doña Triumfa admit to that. I had it dug some time ago. I sent the regular servants away and used imported workmen. I wanted to be prepared, you see."

"So that's where your family is!" Nando remembered his manners and inquired politely, "Doña Triumfa enjoys good health, I hope? And the Señorita Isobel?"

"Doña Triumfa is now fuming. Isobel sulks," chuckled Don Serapio over his shoulder, lifting the candle so that Nando could see the beginning of the steps. "But their health is excellent, thanks to Our Lady. When they heard those footsteps overhead, that veritable army of pounding feet, they neither fumed nor sulked. I can promise you that. They cowered, as did every creole in San Miguel el Grande, and gave thanks for their hiding places."

"But you were one of the instigators," protested Nando, hurrying to keep up with the pattering feet in the darkness. "How did you know that they would turn on the creoles, too?"

"At the time the tunnels were built we didn't think of that. They were intended as a hiding place against the king's soldiers, for they will come, too. But when we heard pounding on the door, and angry voices without—what would you have done?"

Nando felt that no answer was expected, so he made none.

Don Serapio continued on through the house, stopping finally in one of the rooms on the ground floor. Nando could hear him fumbling along the wall, and a moment later he heard the creak of a hinge.

"Perhaps you had better step ahead," suggested the *alcalde*. "When you are inside, I will close the section of wall."

Nando stepped forward, crowding close against the soft, warm person of the creole. Odors of cool, raw earth rushed to meet him from the darkness, closing in even more strongly as the wall slid into place. The flickering candle flame grew steady, shining on the beginnings of a new flight of steps which led down below the house.

"Permit me to go first," said Don Serapio politely, and edged past Nando on the narrow landing.

The steps led to a tunnel, dark, chilly, and lined with heavy beams. Nando could feel their roughness with his hands, and wondered how long it had taken to construct this secret passage underground. He wondered if Isobel had known of its existence. Was this one of the intrigues of which she was so fond of speaking? Somehow he didn't think it was.

Don Serapio stopped suddenly, and Nando could hear his knuckles rapping on hollow wood. This was not the end of the excavation, he was sure, because before the door was opened and he followed the *alcalde* inside, he leaned forward and felt the tunnel extending on into the darkness.

They had come out into a small room, lighted by candles in a heavy silver branched holder. Doña Triumfa, wrapped in a shawl, occupied a straight-backed chair and Isobel sat on a woven blanket on the dirt floor. Doña Triumfa let out a little scream when she saw the white figure behind her husband.

"Don Serapio! One of them has followed you here!" she cried. "Turn and defend yourself."

Don Serapio laughed gently and held his candle close to Nando's face.

"It is a friend, Father Hidalgo's young protégé, Don Fernando. I found him sleeping on the stairs. Like you, I was confused at first, until I looked more closely at his face. Isn't he the clever one to don such a disguise? In the garments of a peon, and with his dark face—bequeathed him no doubt by some Moorish ancestor from Granada," added Don Serapio with quick politeness, "I hardly knew him."

"Fernando de Fuentes," Doña Triumfa reclined her dark head in acknowledgment.

"You sly sneak," accused Isobel bitterly.

"Isobel," chided Doña Triumfa automatically before turning to her husband. "The food, Don Serapio? The food and water you promised to bring from the kitchen?"

The *alcalde* clasped a plump hand to his glistening pink forehead.

"I must confess I forgot them both, señora. In the excitement of viewing the great army which crowds the public square, everything else escaped my mind."

"But we cannot live without food and water!" cried his wife. "It's bad enough to huddle underground like a mole, but even moles venture aboveground on occasion."

"I will go back," promised Don Serapio repentantly. "At once."

"No, let me," volunteered Nando quickly. "I know the way to your kitchen, and I'll be perfectly safe."

"I will go, too." Isobel jumped to her feet, but she sat back down when both her mother and father ordered her to do so.

"It would be safer for you," admitted the *alcalde*. He smiled with appreciation. "And it would be a shame to waste so fine a disguise."

He accompanied Nando up the stairs, and in the darkness manipulated the spring which opened the door. He would stand there, he declared, until the boy returned, then upon an agreed signal he would reopen the door.

"I'll hurry," promised Nando quickly, for Don Serapio had insisted that he carry the single spare candle with him.

"Take what time you need." The *alcalde* settled his person on the step, and in the candlelight Nando could see that he was smiling. "I have much to think about, and in the room below I am given little time to do it."

The kitchen, like the rest of the house, had been turned upside down, and it took Nando only a few moments to discover that the food supplies must have been the first to go. The cupboards stood bare, the shelves empty. Even a few pots and utensils, useful to a soldier who must provide and cook his own food on the march, were missing. But they couldn't deplete the supply of water in the well, so Nando filled a jar.

As he crossed the servant's patio off the kitchen he paused. Clearly Don Serapio was in no hurry, and also he was curious about the goings-on in San Miguel. Had he not dared climb the stairs to the *mirador* to take a look for himself? Anyone who was so desirous for news would not mind a slight delay which might result in more information.

Nando set down his water jar and turned back toward the outside wall. Someone had closed the gate, so he swung it open and stepped outside into the moonlit street. Almost immediately a firm hand grasped him by the shoulder.

"Ah, so we catch another looter!" The grim face of a uniformed soldier peered into his own, but the next moment the hard fingers bruising his shoulder relaxed their grip. "Why, it is Father Hidalgo's servant. He who shared his burro with me on the hot road to Dolores!"

"Jesús Ferías!" gasped Nando in relief. "I'm so glad it is you."

"An act of friendship does not make a soldier forget his responsibility." Once again the fingers closed about his shoulder, but more gently this time. "I am sorry to see you fall so low, Nando. You, of all people, should obey the *cura's* order of no looting in the houses of the creoles."

"But I didn't. I wasn't. You can search me, Jesús. Please search me. You will see that I have stolen nothing," implored Nando quickly.

"Then why were you lurking behind a gate which I myself closed only a few hours ago?" demanded Jesús suspiciously.

"I was trying to find a quiet place where I could stretch out and sleep," improvised Nando quickly. "The square is so crowded. And I remembered the servant's patio here. You know yourself that I spent a night here before. Here by this gate was where I met you the day we went to Dolores."

"That is true," admitted Ferías after a moment's thought. Once more he removed his hand from Nando's shoulder, and this time he kept it away. "It is but natural that you should think of this spot, since the square is, as you say, very crowded. I doubt if one more man could find room to stretch his length."

"Did they—did they hurt anyone?" asked Nando timidly. The matter had been troubling him considerably.

"Oh no." Jesús laughed, brushing away the idea

as absurd. "The *gachupines* are in jail, of course, where they should be. And a few trifles have been taken, which to me is not so bad. We, who will do the fighting, deserve some small reward. But nothing more must be disturbed. The *cura* is quite firm, and the captain has commissioned his men to make sure the orders are carried out. We have closed all the doors to the great houses, and now we patrol the streets."

"And the creoles? Are some of them in jail, too?"

"No." Jesús shook his head in perplexity. "It is a strange thing that most of the creoles should have chosen this day to make journeys elsewhere, but that seems to be the truth. There are none to be found in San Miguel el Grande. At least none of whom I have heard."

"And when they return?" prompted Nando anxiously.

"Why they will return, that's all," Jesús told him in surprise. "To their houses, naturally. None will molest them. They are our allies."

Nando smiled widely. How pleased Don Serapio would be. Doña Triumfa, too. Of Isobel's feelings he was not so certain. Remembering the great scowl of anger which had creased the girl's face, he was not sure if she would ever be pleased at anything again.

"Must I go back to the square, my friend?" he asked Jesús. Then he added coaxingly, "Perhaps if you went with me, the sight of your magnificent uniform would cause one of those who now occupy space to move over and give me room."

"They would not awaken long enough to see my uniform." Jesús laughed, but he was pleased at Nando's evident admiration. "Besides, I cannot leave this street. This is my patrol. Up and down. Down and up. Alert and watchful for looters."

"There will be none. Not with you on guard," declared Nando firmly.

"Of course not." It was the soldier's turn to grow thoughtful. "Perhaps, since I am the guard, and I know you are sleeping behind these walls, it would be all right. You would not steal when you knew there was an armed guard a few feet away."

"On the soul of my blessed mother, I swear it," promised Nando quickly. "On the blue veil of the Virgin likewise."

"Then go," ordered Jesús, smiling. "Enter by the gate and stretch out beside the pepper plants. And may the saints bring you only sweet dreams."

Although Don Serapio protested that he hadn't even noticed the long delay, his round face expressed great relief as he opened the wall for Nando to enter. When the boy had repeated his conversation with the soldier that the creoles were free to re-enter their homes without fear of further intrusion, he was overwhelmingly delighted.

"We must tell Doña Triumfa," he declared. "She and Isobel will be happy to sleep the rest of the night in their own beds. And I will go on down the tunnel and so inform the Conde de la Canal."

"There's no food left in the kitchen," Nando called after him. "And I don't know where your servants are."

The candle flame waved blithely in the darkness ahead. The *alcalde* was far too happy to be concerned with minor items like lack of food or servants.

Nando spent the remainder of the night sleeping in a real bed, and it was late morning before he awoke. He got up and peered through the iron bars of the window. A gardener was carrying buckets of water from the well to sprinkle on the flower beds. He was an old man, and the street sweeper who came through the gate carrying his broom was old, too. Some of the servants must have returned, but only those who were too advanced in age to accompany the army.

Once more Nando put on his cotton garments. After yesterday's march, they were considerably soiled, and he knew that Doña Triumfa would regard them with disapproval, sniffing with her nose, but he had nothing else to wear.

As soon as he appeared on the first floor, Isobel took him in hand. She must have been lying in wait, he decided, but now that the real purpose behind the literary society was out in the open, he had nothing to fear.

"There's breakfast. Of a sort," she told him. "But Papa says we must be thankful to have anything.

Soldiers have to have food to fight, and it's our patriotic duty to share. I'll sit with you while you eat."

She led him to the patio where a small table under a blossoming vine was laid with a white cloth. In a moment a *criada* appeared. On her tray were a cup of chocolate and a tortilla made of rough meal.

"Did you really know the plans the literary society was making?" Isobel wasted no time on preliminaries. As soon as the maid was out of earshot she began her questions.

Nando hesitated. It was a temptation to boast a little, to pretend that he was in the confidence of the leaders, but he decided it was better to tell the truth.

"I didn't even guess."

"At first I thought you knew and wouldn't tell me," she confessed. "I thought you were a specially good liar. But Papa said he was sure that Father Hidalgo would never even drop a hint."

"No. He didn't."

"At least I was right about there being an intrigue." Isobel sighed, unwilling to accept overwhelming defeat. "But when I think that my own papa, whom I thought was so innocent and gullible, was right there in the middle of it—"

Nando swallowed the last of his tortilla and looked hopefully toward the kitchen.

"No more. We have to remember the soldiers'

stomachs," Isobel read his thoughts before continuing. "But now I know where I get my talent for intrigues. From Papa. And from now on I can get my information straight from him without having to go to outsiders."

"Maybe you can." Nando looked at her knowingly. "I bet you didn't even guess there was a tunnel under your house."

"Papa says that was dug over a year ago," she told him with dignity. "We were traveling at the time, the whole family. And a year ago I was only eleven. A year makes a great difference."

"I guess it does," agreed Nando soberly. A year ago he was on the hacienda with his father. There had been no hint of the tragedy and unhappiness which were to come.

"I suppose, since you're wearing those clothes, you're going to try to get into the army." Isobel's eyes narrowed with speculation.

"Of course."

"Does Father Hidalgo know?"

"No. He's been so busy," began Nando vaguely. Then he decided that it was wiser to throw himself on her mercy. "I've been careful to keep out of his way, and of Captain Allende's, too. I thought, when we were far enough away from Dolores so they couldn't send me back—"

"Nando!" From behind, a voice cut the morning air with the sharpness of a spur. "What are you doing here? And dressed like that? Why aren't you at the *cura's* house where we left you?"

They turned in their chairs, staring.

Towering above the plump, amazed *Alcalde* Rodriguez stood Captain Allende. His handsome, smooth-shaven face was flushed with anger, and his narrowed eyes flashed dangerously.

12

"What are you doing here?" repeated Captain Allende, striding across the patio toward the small table where Nando and Isobel were sitting. "And why are you dressed in those ridiculous garments instead of the decent clothes I bought you? Why, you look like a—a—"

"An *Indito?*" said Nando bravely, and raised his head to meet the creole's glare.

The unfortunate slip of the tongue put the captain at a disadvantage. He flushed, and a little of the anger left his voice.

"If I weren't fond of you I wouldn't be so upset,

Nando," he explained awkwardly. "Or if Ramón were here to look after you it would be different. But he isn't, and as his friend I must do what I can to take his place. I presume you followed us from Dolores?"

Nando nodded silently.

"Then this is the end of your travels," declared the captain firmly. "An army—any army—is no place for a thirteen-year-old boy. Last night things almost got beyond our control. Another time our efforts to restrain these people may not be so successful. The larger the army, the more difficult it is to maintain discipline."

"Don Ignacio was just elected lieutenant general of our army," put in the *alcalde*, beaming as proudly as though the honor had been conferred upon himself. "And Father Hidalgo is now captain general. Recruits are pouring in by the minute. You cannot imagine!"

The newly elected lieutenant general brushed aside the matter of his promotion.

"That's why you can't be with us, Nando. No one will have time to look after you."

"I can look after myself."

"No." Allende shook his head firmly. "It's back to Dolores for you."

"Why can't he stay here with us, Papa?" asked Isobel sweetly. "It will be lonesome for Nando in Dolores with Father Hidalgo gone."

"Fernando is always welcome in my house,"

agreed the *alcalde* promptly. "As is any friend of the captain general and his first lieutenant."

"But I don't want to stay here or in Dolores either," protested Nando. "I'm very strong. And I can ride a horse and use a knife and a rope. Doubtless I could fire a gun if I only had one. I don't want to stay behind. I want to fight for our independence, just as you and Ramón will be doing."

A strange look came across Allende's face, and when he spoke his voice was troubled.

"But we do not know on which side your brother will be fighting, Nando. He is with Calleja, the viceroy's general, and the viceroy's men will be our enemies in battle."

"Ramón would never fight against you, Don Ignacio," cried Nando quickly. "You're his best friend."

"Each man must choose his side according to his own conscience," declared the creole quietly. For a moment he was silent, then he assumed an expression of much severity. "But one thing I do know of Ramón. He would want you away from the fighting. So you have your choice, here or in Dolores. Is that understood?"

"Yes, sir," murmured Nando unhappily.

The new lieutenant general smiled; then, giving the two at the table a formal salute, he turned smartly on his heel and started back toward the house. The *alcalde* pattered after him, still beaming proudly.

"Now that," said Isobel, when the two men had

disappeared inside, "was very clever of you, Nando. I didn't know you were so clever."

"Clever?" Nando stared at her resentfully. It was all right for Isobel to be in such cheerful spirits. She hadn't been ordered about like a small child.

"Of course. I listened very carefully to the whole conversation, and you didn't slip once. You let him talk himself out, and then he left without you ever once agreeing to do what he wants."

"But I didn't," protested Nando in amazement. "He told me I had my choice between staying here or going to Dolores. And I—"

"And then he said 'is that understood?' and you said 'yes,'" interrupted Isobel. "You said you understood the choice, but you didn't once say you would abide by it. It leaves you perfectly free to do as you please, and that was very clever."

"I don't think that's what Don Ignacio meant."

"Then he should have been more particular about his words. If he had said 'Do you promise to go to Dolores?' and if you had said 'yes,' you would have to go. But it isn't what he said. I'm a witness, an innocent bystander, and I know." Isobel broke off suddenly. She pulled the long, reddish-brown braid which hung down her back over her shoulder and studied it thoughtfully. "Do you think, if I cut my hair and dressed in men's clothes, it would be enough of a disguise so I could go with you?"

Nando ignored her question.

"You mean, I'm not to pay any attention to Don Ignacio? That I'm to go with the army?"

"Of course." She frowned as though Nando were a slow-thinking child for whom she had no more patience. "Well, what about it? Would cutting off my hair be enough of a disguise?"

"Certainly not," he declared vehemently. "You wouldn't fool a soul. And besides, even if I do decide to go, I wouldn't take you."

"You're probably right. I couldn't get away with it," she said after a moment. "I couldn't be an *Indito* because of my freckles. And there are so few creole officers that they'd find me out right away. Well, you'll just have to go by yourself."

"I still haven't decided whether I will or not," he insisted stubbornly. "It doesn't seem quite right."

"Oh, you'll go. It's very exciting. Almost like an intrigue. And you don't have to stay. In fact, I don't want you to stay. You must come back here and report to me everything that's been going on."

"That settles it!" Nando stood up angrily, almost upsetting the small table. "I'm not going!"

"I think you'd better let them get a head start," mused Isobel, ignoring him completely. "After the first day or two, Captain—I mean Lieutenant General Allende will never think to look for you. I've read that an army moves slowly. You can catch up easily enough on a burro."

Early the next morning the army departed for Celaya, and four days later Nando set out astride a burro. Isobel had filled a straw bag with food for his journey, much to the amusement of her father.

"One would think that Fernando intended to travel for a week instead of the twenty miles from here to Dolores," he declared.

Nando hung his head. He disliked deceiving the plump, good-natured *alcalde*, but Isobel had been very firm about it. Don Serapio would never have permitted the boy to follow the army. He could not understand why Nando wanted to return to Dolores, but he put nothing in his way.

Outside of Nando's regrets over deceiving Don Serapio he felt only eagerness for the adventure ahead of him. He had wanted to be with the army all the time. Thirteen was not too young to fight for the independence of one's country, no matter what anyone said. Only Isobel understood. She was an extraordinarily bright girl. Why, the way she had seized upon the loophole in Nando's conversation with Don Ignacio was worthy of any *licenciado*. It was too bad she had been born a girl so she couldn't be one.

The road from San Miguel el Grande to Celaya wound westward some thirty miles through lands ordinarily given over to agriculture. Nando had not gone far before he was thankful for the food Isobel had provided. Every edible crop had been stripped from the vines or dug from the earth by the liberators. Women and children were already working in the ravished fields, stoically attempting to replant where they could. Since it was doubtful that there would be any rain before next summer, Nando feared that there would be many empty stomachs in the months ahead.

But if the farms were a sorry sight, Celaya, when he reached there, was even worse. The forces had come and gone, and the results of their stay were evident on every hand. Some buildings had been partially torn down, ashes of fires made ugly scars upon the square, and the streets were littered with rubble. Scavengers probed among the debris, and because they were the only people in sight Nando reluctantly approached one of them.

"Oh yes. They have gone." The old man looked up, smirking. His gums were blue and swollen, devoid of teeth. "They went to Guanajuato, fifty miles to the north. Celaya is a poor town, but Guanajuato is rich. It has the mines, you know. Silver. Ah, what I wouldn't give to pick over the leavings of such a city!"

Nando's stomach churned with revulsion, but he tried to keep his tone civil.

"But what happened here? I thought that the army only intended to imprison the *gachupines,* not wreck the town."

"Our *gachupines* resisted," the old man told him proudly. "Naturally, they had to be killed. And once an army begins to kill—after all, fifty thousand men are hard to control."

"Fifty thousand!" repeated Nando incredulously.

It seemed hard to believe, but now he remembered that only women and children had worked the fields, and there were no young men among the scavengers on the streets. Wherever the army went, able-bodied men must have flocked to follow the banner from Atotonilco's sanctuary.

"That's what they say." The old man stared speculatively at Nando's burro. "That is a fine animal. Where did you get it?"

"It's mine," Nando told him hastily and pulled on the rope to lead the burro away.

He did not stay in Celaya any longer. He did not like what he saw there, and besides, if he meant to follow the army to Guanajuato he had better get started. It was a long distance. He could not make it in a single day.

Once again he found he could follow the route of the army by the conditions of the countryside, only now things grew even worse. Fifty thousand men required many times the food needed by a couple of thousand. No chickens remained to scratch around the occasional Indian huts, and whenever he saw the great trampling of a new-sprouted field, Nando guessed that it must belong to some hacienda whose owner was suspect.

The going was even slower than he had expected. He was in the mountains now, and both he and the burro grew tired of climbing up and up, then making a perilous descent only to renew the climb. He rationed his food, mentally thanking Isobel for having provided so generously, but even so his supply gave out. For the first time he began to doubt her wisdom in letting him wait so long before setting out. Isobel had been sure he would overtake the army, since he was traveling alone and had a burro to ride when he was tired. But this army traveled rapidly, wiping everything clean as it went.

He came that evening to an hacienda and stopped, hoping to beg a little food. The army had camped here before him. He could see their signs, the ashes of cooking fires, the trodden fields, the inevitable litter everywhere. But at least they had not wrecked the house and buildings, and he went timidly to the back.

An Indian girl answered his rap, and to his amazement did not seem surprised to see him.

"Another recruit," she decided, smiling. "They are growing younger all the time. But at least you have a burro. That will be of help. Come inside."

Nando stepped thankfully through the doorway and sat on the floor where she pointed. The girl resumed her chore of washing dishes, which he had obviously interrupted.

"You are a day late," she chided. "But perhaps you are from some distance, and the news of this opportunity to help throw off the cruel yoke of our oppressors was slow in reaching you. What is your name?"

"Nando."

"I am Teresa," she announced. "I peel vegetables

for the cook, and pound maize, and wash the dishes when the *patrón* has finished his meal."

"Where is the cook?" Nando looked about him hopefully as he patted his empty stomach. "And who is your *patrón?*"

"The cook does not linger when her work for the day is finished," Teresa told him condescendingly. "And this is the Hacienda de Burras. Oh, we have had great excitement here I can tell you. For two days the army of the liberators has been camped here. The captain general and the lieutenant general and some of the other officers stayed in this very house, under the same roof which shelters you now. They left only this morning."

"Where have they gone?"

"They left for Guanajuato. They waited, you understand, for the return of their messengers. They sent two men, finely dressed officers, to the *Intendente* Riano. They demanded of him the surrender of the city. And can you imagine the reply of that foolish *gachupín?*"

"He refused?"

"He replied that he would defend the city with his life!" Teresa's eyes flashed indignantly, while her stiff scrubbing brush moved up and down against the sides of a cooking pot. "He has moved all the *gachupines,* with their wives and families, into the *Alhondiga de Granaditas,* and there he means to make a stand."

"What is that?" asked Nando.

"The warehouse," frowned Teresa impatiently. "For storing grain, stupid."

Perhaps she would have said more but the pink rays of sunset which had been entering through the open doorway were suddenly blocked out, leaving the kitchen dusky with shadows.

From his corner, Nando looked up quickly. A man was standing in the opening, his features invisible against the bright sky. As he moved forward into the room and the light came with him, Nando could see that he was young. He had dark hair and a pleasantly smiling face with blunt Indian features. The remarkable thing about him was his shoulders. They were so wide they strained the seams of his long cotton shirt, and below the short sleeves his arm muscles stood out like ropes. Since he was unusually short, the massive shoulders and powerful arms gave him a curious top-heavy appearance.

"El Pipila!" exclaimed Teresa in delight. She rushed forward to embrace the stranger, and her scrubbing brush trailed a stream of soapy water down his back.

El Pipila meant hen turkey, thought Nando. A curious name for a young man who looked so capable of taking care of himself.

"What are you doing here, El Pipila?" demanded Teresa, finally letting him go. "Why are you not working in the mines as always?"

"The mines are closed. Have you not heard there is to be a battle? Of course I shall take part. I came only to receive my mother's blessing, because after this battle is won I shall leave with the army of liberators."

"We shall be so proud of you," cried Teresa joyfully. Her eyes fell on the forgotten Nando sitting in the corner and she smiled, including him in the conversation. "Here is another who wishes to fight for freedom. His name is Nando. He is young, but he has a burro. This is my cousin Juan José Amaro Barajas. We call him El Pipila."

Nando rose to his feet and saluted the stranger gravely.

"I am most honored, señor."

El Pipila laughed good-naturedly.

"Save such formality for the great ones, boy. You are young to be a soldier."

"Thirteen," said Nando defensively.

"That is not young after all," declared El Pipila. "I was working in the mines long before that. Well, Teresa, what have you for two hungry soldiers to eat?"

"Two cold tortillas only." Her voice was not only sad but a little reluctant.

"Which you had saved out for yourself as a bedtime snack, no doubt," decided El Pipila severely. "It's not much, but hand it over. We must eat to have strength to fight tomorrow. Eh, Nando?"

13

"Behold," declared El Pipila dramatically. "Guanajuato lies below you!"

As though able to understand the invitation to pause, the burro which Nando was riding stopped short while the boy peered down into the deep chasm below.

The city was crowded into a narrow, deep ravine and the dwellings were erected on terraces rising from four sides. From this spot on the road, which descended perilously down the mountain, it looked like some plaything sold at Christmas for children. Miniature trees grew beside toy houses, the whole surrounded by fragile walls that looked like cardboard. There were tiny domed churches, and a gray castlelike building which might have housed tin soldiers. Through the center of town trickled a little stream, like a silver ribbon.

"The *Alhondiga*," announced El Pipila, his square finger singling out the castle. "A veritable fortress, I can assure you. It is there that the *Intendente* Riano, with the other *gachupines*, have taken their stand. And it is there that we will fight our battle. Follow me."

He set off down the road at an untiring dogtrot, and Nando kicked the burro with his sandals as a signal to follow.

He was not too happy about El Pipila. True, it was well to enter Guanajuato with someone who knew his way around, but Nando wanted to do things his own way. He was prepared, even anxious, to fight for the independence of his country, but he would have preferred to do so from the back of a horse, and with proper weapons. As it was, he had no weapons at all, not even a stick. So far as he could see, neither had El Pipila, yet the ex-miner was ready to enter the ranks of battle immediately.

The closer they came, the less Guanajuato looked like a toy village. It was a real city, Nando saw, and a rich one, too, for there were many three-storied houses with carved doorways and iron-barred windows. There were imposing government buildings, towered churches, with domes of polychrome tile, fountains, and tree-shaded plazas. He had only a hazy impression of these things, however, for El Pipila kept hurrying him on. He trotted ahead, pausing often to wait, and shouting impatient insults at the burro before starting on again.

The miner knew his way around the city, and must have taken advantage of every shortcut, for before long they were in sight of the liberating army.

"Leave your burro," ordered El Pipila. "He can be of no use to you for a while."

"But I don't want to lose him," protested Nando.

"What is one burro? There is always another."

El Pipila frowned, extending one huge hand. Before he knew what was happening, Nando found his feet on the cobblestones. The next minute, El Pipila had him by the wrist and was dragging him forward into the crowd.

There was no organized assault upon the stone warehouse where the Spaniards had taken their stand. The majority of besiegers were untrained, and each man did any task which occurred to him at the moment. Ahead of them Nando could hear gunfire, and occasionally the louder booms of cannon rose above the shouting of the crowd.

"We can see nothing from here," decided El Pipila in disgust. "Let us go back, climb up a few terraces. I wish to know what is going on."

He turned and plowed his way back through the crowd, dragging Nando after him.

As the miner had said, from the terraced streets above they had a better view. But they had to go even higher than he had intended, for the soldiers were stationed on the first streets facing the *Alhondiga*. Here their muskets could fire on the head of any Spaniard that appeared above the ramparts of the granary roof.

"There's Father Hidalgo." Nando's eyes had searched first for his friend. The *cura* was riding up and down on his horse, while the peons moved aside to give him room. "He shouldn't be there in the open. He should be farther back, out of the way."

"A good general does not direct from the rear, but from the front. It gives courage to his men," declared El Pipila. "Even the *gachupines* know that. See, their *intendente* directs his men on the roof."

Nando had already seen the armed Spaniards on the roof of the fortress. It was their guns which had caused his alarm for Father Hidalgo's safety.

"Which is the *intendente?*" he asked.

"He wears a blue plume, the arrogant one." El Pipila spit on the street to show his disapproval. "See, now he pokes out his head to view the street. You may see him clearly."

At that instant the gun of one of Allende's men found its mark, and the blue plume, which had been leaning from the ledge above the rooftop, quivered, then disappeared behind the stones. A great cheer went up from the street.

"They killed him! They killed the *intendente!*" gasped Nando. His stomach felt cold and shuddery.

"A great stroke of luck," gloated El Pipila. "Without a leader, what will the *gachupines* do now?"

Clearly the loss of their leader had created great confusion among the ranks of the defenders. The firing from the rooftop and the windows ceased. Nando could see the figure of Lieutenant General Allende as he left his soldiers on the terrace and hurried down to confer with his general.

In a few minutes someone raised a white flag from the roof of the *Alhondiga,* but even before it had time to flutter twice, someone else from the rooftop had jerked it down.

"Aha," cried El Pipila in delight. "Confusion among the *gachupines!* Now there is nothing to do but to take the building itself. We are through with the guns that go bang, bang. The fighting will be as it should be, man to man."

"Where are you going?" cried Nando, for it was plain that the miner was about to leave him.

"I go to do what I have come to do. To fight," El Pipila told him. He hesitated, then said swiftly, "Remain here, Nando. You are after all still a child, and battles are not for children. Your time will come."

He turned and started down the winding street at his usual tireless trot, and Nando stared after him with hurt eyes. What had he said or done to cause El Pipila to regard him as a child? Last night the miner had claimed that thirteen was not too young to fight, but now he calmly reversed his decision.

For a moment Nando considered following anyway, but common sense told him to stay where he was. If the beggar in Celaya was right, there were already over fifty thousand grown men surrounding the building, and most of them had been unable as yet to make themselves useful.

Below, the fighting had begun again, only this time it was of a different nature. There were several lower gates and doors in the *Alhondiga*, and rebel groups were attempting to storm each in turn. Every time they were driven back by the gunfire which came through the iron bars in the windows, and Nando could see that casualties were beginning to pile up.

Then there seemed to be a lull. The raids on the doors were given up as futile. Standing back out of range of fire, he could see Father Hidalgo and Allende, who seemed to be conferring, deciding between them what to try next. And then—Nando rubbed his eyes—they were joined by a third man in the white cotton garments of a peon. He was shorter by a head than either of the two creoles, but he had wide shoulders. As he walked, he was slightly bent under the weight of a huge, flat gray stone.

It was El Pipila, Nando's companion since yesterday, who had come weaponless to fight. But now he had a weapon, if that was to be the use of the stone.

The three men stood talking for a moment, and it looked to Nando as though El Pipila was explaining something. He put the stone on the ground beside him and leaned on it with one elbow, gesturing with the other hand. After a moment, Father Hidalgo nodded his head. He appeared to call out, although Nando could not be sure of that for the distance was too great to hear.

A soldier came running with a lighted torch. El Pipila got down on his hands and knees, and Allende and the soldier placed the stone slab on his back, tying it in place. Then, with the handle of the lighted torch in his teeth, El Pipila began to crawl forward toward the *Alhondiga*.

Nando held his breath. He knew now what the miner meant to do. The main entrance was a great double wooden door, flanked by several windows. His plan must be to set it on fire, to burn it to the ground so that the insurgents could rush through. The heavy stone was protection from the lead, sure to pour down on him from every window. It was a brave thing to do, a deed which required steady nerves and a strong back. Nando was proud to call El Pipila his friend.

The noisy crowd grew as silent as though they were attending Mass. Even those on the outskirts, who could not see, were quiet. They had been told what was happening, and they waited to hear the outcome of this daring venture. Occasionally a jeering voice called through one of the barred windows, warning El Pipila what would happen when the first burst of gunfire hit the slab of rock. But El Pipila crawled on, unheeding.

As he reached the gate, the barrage of bullets began. Some of them spattered against the slab, making it rock from side to side. When that happened the miner stopped a second, waiting for the rolling to cease, before he crawled on.

He was at the gate now, and the gunfire was even more intense. It ricocheted against the rock on El Pipila's back, striking dirt and dust from the cobblestones all about him. But the ropes still held, and the torch still burned. He was holding it now against a corner of the door, willing the dry wood to catch spark and burn. Nando willed it, too, and prayed hard for the help of every saint he had ever heard mentioned.

When El Pipila began inching backward out of the way of the flames, the crowd knew of his success and let out a mighty cheer that echoed back and forth against the surrounding slopes. They could see the fire now as it crawled up the gate, eating deep into the old wood. But of equal importance to them was the hero who had set the blaze.

El Pipila turned, balancing the heavy stone slab on his mighty shoulders and began crawling back toward them. As soon as he had covered half the

distance, a dozen men, disregarding possible danger
to themselves, ran to meet him. They untied the
stone, helped him to his feet, and joyfully went
together to greet their general.

By this time Nando was literally jumping up and
down with excitement. For a moment he wondered
if El Pipila would come back to him here on the
terrace. Then he realized that the hero would have
no thought for someone he regarded as a child. El
Pipila was one of the liberators now, and with them
he would go on to conquer the city.

Nando considered going down there himself and
then decided against it. He had no weapons, and
unlike El Pipila he did not know how to use what
was at hand.

Before long the wooden gates burned through
and the insurgent army poured into the *Alhondiga*.
Nando could no longer see what was going on, and
it made him uneasy. He thought he heard women
screaming, and certainly there was a great deal of
noise.

After due time the army reappeared, and now
they began surging in and out of the surrounding
houses. There was no mistaking the screams this
time, and Nando grew cold with helpless horror.
Father Hidalgo, Allende and his officers rode up
and down the streets, shouting commands to halt
the killing, to cease the looting and excesses, but
to no avail. Even the soldiers, who in San Miguel
el Grande had patrolled the streets, ignored their

officers. They were as bad as any of the others.

When Nando saw that the mob was slowly swarming up the terraces and would soon reach the street where he stood, he turned and began to run. He did not fear for himself. A dirty Indian boy would have nothing to steal. The worst he could expect was to be kicked out of the way. But he wasn't an Indian boy. He was a creole gentleman, and he felt sick. He had never felt so sick before.

As soon as he could locate it, Nando took the road out of town which he and El Pipila had traveled earlier that day. He had resolved to return to San Miguel el Grande, because he had no other place to go. Don Serapio had said he was welcome anytime, and Nando hoped the *alcalde* had been speaking the truth.

He had completely lost his appetite, but knowing that it would return tomorrow he stopped at the Hacienda de Burras. In exchange for his account of the extraordinary exploits of her cousin, El Pipila, Teresa was happy to load him down with cold tortillas as provisions for his trip. In addition, she gave him something of almost greater value, information concerning a shorter road than the one he had taken before through Celaya. Since this road ran through Dolores, Nando decided to stop there for the fine clothes Don Ignacio had bought for him. He was tired of being mistaken for a peon.

Concha was glad to see him when he arrived three days later, tired and very hungry, although she scolded him soundly for his disobedience in following the army. But her curiosity got the better of her, and as soon as Nando was finished with his hot bath she sat at the table opposite and demanded news of the battle at Guanajuato.

It was the first time Nando had told the whole story. Teresa had only wanted to hear of El Pipila, and to be assured of the final victory. Concha listened to the whole thing, the killings which followed, the pillage of the houses, and her stolid Indian face was without expression.

"It makes you sad," she said soberly, when he fell silent. "You blame the peons for killing the whites and for stealing their property. But have you stopped to think that for three hundred years this has been going on in reverse? Sometimes a man cannot help but store bitterness in his soul for the wrongs he has suffered. And this bitterness is often passed on to his sons. Think of that, Nando. Think carefully before you condemn."

She rose and started from the room, then suddenly turned back.

"It had slipped my mind. A letter came for you while you were gone, and one for the *cura* by the same messenger. I will fetch them."

Nando knew even before she handed him the folded paper, sealed with the arms of de Fuentes impressed in the wax, that it was from Alejandro. The answer to Father Hidalgo's letter had finally come. Well, this time Nando was ready for it. He was willing to enter the priesthood or anything else Alejandro wished him to do.

But the letter, in Alejandro's careful penmanship, did not even mention school or being a priest. Instead it urged Nando to come home, back to the hacienda. Alejandro had been thinking things over and had decided that he had done a great injustice to his brother by asking him to leave his home, which was obviously so dear to him, and enter a profession about which he cared nothing. He begged Nando's pardon deeply for this wrong he had done and prayed that he would return by the first *diligencia*. The same trusted messenger who carried this letter and the one to the *cura*, thanking him for his kindnesses, would deliver a box. It contained gold to cover any necessary expenses of travel. Alejandro hoped that his brother would put it to the use for which it was intended as soon as possible.

Nando felt a happy glow come over him as he read the letter through. Alejandro was no longer ashamed of him. He wanted him to come home, back where he belonged, to the life which was his birthright.

He looked up at Concha standing impassively before him.

"Where is the box?" he asked. "The one left by the messenger who brought the letters?"

"Box?" she repeated in surprise. "He left no box. Only the two letters. He handed them to me at the door, then he got on his horse and rode away."

14

It was the second of November when Nando returned to San Miguel el Grande, and all around the plaza vendors were displaying those special items which are reserved for the Day of the Dead. There were flowers to be carried to the cemetery, of course, and creamy yellow candles to be lighted on the graves at twilight. But there were also candies, patiently molded at home in the shape of vegetables, red tomatoes, brown *jicimas*, green peppers, and candy fruit in the form of bananas and oranges and limes. There were sugar animals, sheep and bulls and burros, each an exquisite work of art, as well as many white candy skulls, because on this day one must not forget the earthly remains of the spirit which has gone to dwell among the angels.

At any other time Nando would have stopped to inspect these tempting wares spread out on *sarapes* on the ground before each kneeling vendor. Today he gave them only a passing glance as he pushed through the crowds of bargainers. He was on his way to the house of the *Alcalde* Rodriguez, and he had not yet made up his mind what he would say when he arrived.

Should he show them Alejandro's letter? Or would they think it just a plea for sympathy? Since the box containing money had not been delivered, would Don Serapio feel it was only courtesy to finance Nando's journey out of his own pocket? It would require the purchase of a horse, and horses were very expensive. Moreover, he had already loaned a burro, which Nando had promptly lost. How could he explain that? He didn't want to say that the animal had been left behind at Guanajuato, for then Don Serapio would know that he hadn't spent his time at Dolores. Perhaps it would have been better had he remained at the house of Father Hidalgo. But he didn't want to do that. He liked the servants well enough, but now Nando wanted to be with his own class, to wear the silk garments which he carried done up in a cloth under his arm.

He reached the great door under the two carved

cherubs and resolutely pulled on the bell rope. At least he would have Isobel to help him parry the polite questions of Don Serapio and Doña Triumfa. Maybe Isobel could even think of a plausible explanation for the loss of the burro.

The *criada* who opened the door peered carefully into his face. Then she allowed him to enter without delay.

"The *patrón* is in the *sala de recibo*," she told him. "Also the doña and Señorita Isobel. They spoke with a messenger, who left only a few minutes ago."

Nando walked down the hallway and stood hesitating at the open doorway of the parlor for receiving guests. Inside he could hear three voices, all speaking at once and in great excitement, as though each was delivering a monologue for his own benefit.

Isobel saw him first. She jumped up from the carved stool on which she had been sitting and rushed forward.

"Nando! How nice you came back." Her voice carried a warning tone which he could not miss. "A messenger has just been here. He came from Guanajuato. Of course you could not have heard, having been in Dolores all this time, but our army has won a great victory."

"Indeed yes, my boy." The *alcalde* bustled forward. "Sit down. Let me tell you all about it before I go out to spread the news."

Doña Triumfa looked up from her embroidery, and her eyes lighted on the cloth bundle under Nando's arm.

"Perhaps our young friend would prefer to change first into proper clothing. This time you brought more suitable garments, Fernando?"

"Yes, señora," Nando assured her quickly.

"He can do that later," protested Don Serapio. "Great news, my boy. Great news. The city of Guanajuato has fallen. The captain general, our Father Hidalgo, has established an *ayuntamiento*, a council of loyal creoles, who has declared our independence. He has opened the mint, and is making coins of silver from the mines. We will need funds, you understand, to carry on this fight. And he has established a foundry, which will construct cannon. Our forces will need those, too."

Nando listened with amazement. These were fine things, necessary things for the war effort, but as he well knew they were not all of the story.

"Were there any casualties?" he asked cautiously. "Was anyone hurt?"

"The messenger made no report on that," admitted Don Serapio in a surprised voice. "And I forgot to ask. Of course there must have been a few. It is a rare victory which is won with no bloodshed. The important thing is that we were victorious. Now I must go tell the others, the Conde de la Canal, the Lámbarri brothers—" His voice trailed after him as he trotted briskly out of the room and down the entranceway.

"You look very dusty, Fernando," observed Doña Triumfa. "Perhaps now you would like a bath?"

"It's a dusty road from Dolores," said Isobel quickly. "One can grow very dirty in twenty miles, riding a burro."

"About the burro," said Nando unhappily. "I'm afraid I lost it."

"Of no matter," said Doña Triumfa with quick politeness.

"What's one burro?" declared Isobel airily, and Nando remembered that El Pipila had used those same words in Guanajuato. She began steering him from the room. "I will tell one of the maids about Nando's bath, Mama, and when he has dressed himself in proper clothing, perhaps he will return and tell us the news of Dolores."

"Very good," agreed Doña Triumfa absently, tying a fresh knot in her embroidery thread.

When they were out of earshot, Isobel turned to Nando with shining eyes.

"I can hardly wait to hear," she confessed. "Your story of the battle will be much better than the messenger's, I know."

"It was awful," he told her unhappily. "Except for El Pipila. He was magnificent. And I'm sorry about the burro. I just couldn't go back and get him."

"Don't worry about the burro. I'll make up something. The stupid things are always wandering away, anyhow. Now go have your bath before Mama begins to wonder. Later I'll make an opportunity so you can tell me about everything."

The opportunity did not come until early evening. Unlike the peons who spent the whole of the Day of the Dead, and half of the night, sitting on the graves of their departed relatives, the Rodriguez family did not visit the cemetery until twilight. At that time, Don Serapio dismounted from his carriage with great dignity and placed an armload of poinsettia and a lighted candle at the final resting-place of his ancestors. The peons, who had been chattering and visiting with their neighbors who sat on nearby graves, were silent while the carriage bearing the creoles was nearby. But as soon as it rolled away their conversations and the picnic suppers they had been consuming were continued.

Although she had not even descended from the carriage, Doña Triumfa was much affected by the expedition. She declared that it had left her with a headache, and as soon as they returned home she went to her room. Don Serapio was also exhausted. He had visited the household of every important creole in San Miguel el Grande, repeating the glorious news from Guanajuato. He went to bed, too, and Nando was free to recount his adventures to Isobel, who promptly dismissed the servants so that they could be alone.

At first he had thought to spare her the ending,

since, after all, she was a girl. But Isobel wouldn't let him. She insisted on hearing everything, and the gray eyes grew large in her round, freckled face as she listened.

"That isn't nice. It's not nice at all," she declared when he was finished. Then she added thoughtfully, "Papa was even wiser than I thought to build a tunnel. I think I'll stay right here until the war is over. And perhaps you'd better stay, too, Nando."

"But I'm going home. I'm wanted there." This was the time to display Alejandro's letter, and he held it out to her.

Isobel took a long time with her reading. Perhaps it was because the stars gave so little light in the patio where they were sitting. When she looked up, her face was thoughtful.

"This letter was written long before the start of the war. Your brother can't have known it was going to happen, or he wouldn't have told you to come home by yourself. I'm afraid you'll have to stay. For all I know, there's not even a *diligencia* to Puebla any more."

"I've thought of that," admitted Nando. "But I know the way. At least I think I remember. The problem is finding a horse to ride."

"I suppose you could buy one." Her voice sounded a little regretful.

"That's the trouble. The box of gold Alejandro writes about wasn't delivered with the letters."

"This is war," Isobel reminded him quickly. In

the starlight her smile grew very bright. "War does funny things to people. It makes them act in a way they would never think of doing in normal times. You saw that yourself in Guanajuato. The trusted messenger wasn't so trustworthy after all."

"I'm afraid not." Nando sighed. "But I'll still need a horse to get home. I hate to suggest it, but do you suppose your father could loan— After all, Alejandro would pay him back."

"Oh no," cried Isobel quickly. "You mustn't ask Papa to loan you the money for a horse. He can't afford it. He is very short of money just now. You don't think those special messengers ride here from the battles for nothing, do you? They have to be paid, and it's very costly."

"Of course." Nando was embarrassed that he should have even made the suggestion.

"It would be better if you didn't even mention receiving the letter," she finished earnestly. "Because then Papa would feel that he had to offer to do something, even if we all had to go hungry to pay for it."

"I won't say a word," promised Nando. "Not a word."

The days passed slowly, monotonously, broken only by the occasional messengers who reached San Miguel el Grande with news from the outside. The messengers were slow and the news was always outdated by the time it arrived, but they received it avidly, studying each single item carefully and piecing the whole together as best they could.

The liberating army was now marching on Mexico City, one hundred thirty-four miles away. That it would capture the capital as easily as it had conquered Guanajuato they had no doubt. . . . The army had arrived at Monte de las Cruces, within twenty-five miles of its goal, and there it had encountered a Spanish force under General Torcuato de Trujilla. The liberators had eighty thousand men and the Spaniards but three thousand, yet the royalists were trained to warfare. Moreover they had horses, guns, artillery, everything which went to make up modern warfare. It was whispered that there was a difference of opinion between the captain general and the lieutenant general before the battle. Allende wished to withhold his undisciplined troops and act on the defensive, but the *cura* believed they could win by numbers and ordered the battle to begin.

It was a glorious thing—costly, because so many Indians gave their lives. Why, they even tried to stop cannon balls with their sombreros! But Allende was like a lion in his bravery. At the head of his own company he charged a mountain and captured the enemy's artillery. The Spanish gave way. The army of the viceroy was demoralized. It fled back to the city!

Everyone was very excited over the report of this triumph. They sang in the streets, and the creoles toasted one another at dinner. But their celebrations were premature, for in a few days another messenger arrived with news which was not so pleasant.

Father Hidalgo had marched his army to within fifteen miles of Mexico City, and then stopped. He sent a demand to the viceroy for surrender, but when there was no reply, he turned his forces around and marched back toward the Provinces Internas.

No one knew why he had reached this decision. It was said that it was made in the face of the lieutenant general's protests, that Allende wished to attack the city. Some claimed it was because spies had reported to Father Hidalgo that the city was well provisioned and could withstand long siege. Others said that he had intercepted a dispatch which said that General Calleja was coming from San Luis Potosí. While others whispered—but this the good people of San Miguel could not believe—that the *cura* dreaded witnessing the excesses he had seen in Guanajuato.

But there were other disturbing bits of news. The Church had again accused Father Hidalgo of heresy. The *Inquisición* had reopened his closed file, and this time there was no one to defend him. The rumor was that the *Licenciado* Hidalgo had lost his wits; that he had gone mad, doubtless from strain and worry over the behavior of his brother.

To offset the banner carried by the liberators, which bore the picture of the Virgin of Guadalupe, the viceroy had sent to the mountain shrine of Totoltepec. From there he had taken the Virgin de los Remedios, a small doll-like image which had once brought success to the *Conquistadores*. It was carried to the great cathedral in Mexico City, and there proclaimed *generalissimo* of the king's army. This was a bad, worrisome thing to the liberators, for the Virgin de los Remedios was very sacred.

After that there were no messengers for a long time. No one knew, or could even guess, how the war was going. They did not even know where it was being fought.

Then late one afternoon, when the grackles were beginning to wing into the leafy trees above the plaza, a small detachment of men marched into town.

At first glance it did not look like a company of soldiers, for it was headed by a robed priest riding a mule, and the men who followed wore the soiled white cotton jackets and trousers of peons. It was their marching which gave them away. They walked two by two, keeping step with each other, their eyes straight ahead, and they did not carry on aimless conversations as do men in peacetime.

Don Serapio had been sitting on one of the iron benches in the plaza, taking the air. As soon as he recognized the significance of the group, he jumped to his feet and hurried forward to address the leader. As the result of a few pointed questions, the *alcalde* invited the whole company to his house, the leader to take dinner with the family, the others to share the servants' meal in the kitchen patio.

Nando met the priest as soon as the *alcalde* ushered him inside the door.

"This is Lieutenant General José María Morelos," introduced Don Serapio, beaming with pride. "He was a former pupil of Father Hidalgo—I mean of our captain general—at the college of St. Nicolás in Valladolid."

Nando bowed, making the required response to the introduction, but his eyes were busy inspecting the newcomer.

The man, who wore the robes of a priest from some humble parish, was a *mestizo,* and his unusually dark skin and thick lips hinted at a strain of African ancestry. He was very short, barely five feet tall, and from beneath his cowled hood straggled straight, coarse black hair. He had sharp, unsmiling eyes, which regarded them each in turn.

"We are most honored, señor," said Doña Triumfa in a tone which belied her words. "Will you please select the seat which finds the most favor in your eyes?"

Morelos chose a hard-seated straight chair, and when he sat his long, dusty robes spread all around him on the rich carpet.

"Tell us the news," begged Don Serapio. "How is the health of our illustrious captain general?"

"Father Hidalgo has now been proclaimed the *generalissimo,*" corrected the priest. "And Allende

has been named captain general. Their health, praise
be to God, continues good."

"Splendid!" crowed the *alcalde*. "*Generalissimo!*
Well, well!"

"You have just left them, señor?" inquired Doña
Triumfa politely.

"Not two days ago. The scouts reported that General Calleja was coming with ten thousand men. A
battle was inevitable. And so I took my company
and left while the others were taking up positions
to meet the enemy."

"You left?" gasped Don Serapio. "You cannot
mean that you deserted?"

Lieutenant General Morelos's lips curved politely
but his eyes remained unsmiling.

"I had my orders from the *generalissimo*. I am
to take these twenty-five men to the regions south
of Mexico City. There I am to recruit a new army
and await instructions. Father Hidalgo wished that
I leave as soon as possible, and let nothing stand
in my way. I am drilling the men as we proceed,
instructing them in military matters and trying to
instill a sense of discipline. These things are lacking
in the army of the *generalissimo*. There are so many
men, too few officers. It is a great handicap."

Relief showed plainly on the *alcalde*'s pink face.
For a moment he had been afraid he had invited
a coward to dinner.

"And where is this place selected for the next

encounter with our enemy? Where do our brave troops await the army of General Calleja?"

"Not far from here. They were taking their stand at the Hacienda Marfil, only a few miles from the city of Guanajuato."

Nando, who had been listening carefully, sat forward in his chair, his eyes glued on Morelos's face. He did not even notice Doña Triumfa frown and try to signal him that he was guilty of rude staring at a guest.

"It is becoming the fashion for priests to take up arms, it seems." Since she could not attract Nando's attention, Doña Triumfa did her best to distract the visitor with conversation. "First Father Hidalgo, now you."

"We never know to what service we may be called, señora," he told her simply. "I was the *cura* of a small parish in Carácuaro. I presented myself to the *generalissimo* with the request that he use me as chaplain. But he told me they had too many chaplains. He said I would make a better general than a priest, and so I obey his wishes. I will do the best I can. I would give the last drop of my blood for the freedom of my country."

Doña Triumfa's smile was a little warmer than before.

"Let us go in to dinner," she invited.

When Isobel jostled him to attention, Nando arose and followed the others, but he heard little of the conversation at dinner. The last he had heard of his brother, Ramón had been with General Calleja. And Calleja was expected at Guanajuato. Less than fifty miles away, he kept telling himself over and over. At this very minute, Ramón is less than fifty miles away!

15

Dinner had been served at two o'clock, and at its conclusion everyone observed the *siesta,* a rest during the heat of the day. Morelos's twenty-five men lay on the stones of the servant's patio, their sombreros shading their faces, but the little priest-turned-general was shown to one of the upper rooms where he could sleep in greater comfort.

Nando had remained in his chair throughout the meal under the greatest duress. The news Morelos had brought filled him with excitement.

A dozen times he reminded himself that Ramón might no longer be with General Calleja's troops.

Many of the former creole officers had deserted to fill posts among the opposition. A few had gone over for selfish reasons, since it meant a big increase in rank. Others had been influenced by the issues at stake, and having lived in the Rodriguez household, Nando had come to accept these demands of justice as only right. It seemed to him that every creole should feel that way.

Ramón had very likely accepted them long ago, and was even now fighting side by side with his old comrade, Don Ignacio. But still—what if the true nature of the revolt had been concealed from Calleja's officers? What if Ramón had been filled with lies? It was Nando's duty to find his brother and explain matters. The two of them had always been able to talk things out. He could make Ramón understand. He knew he could.

To reach the Hacienda Marfil in time to overtake the army meant that he had to have a good horse. A burro would not do this time. And his only hope of securing one was to take Isobel into his confidence.

He cornered her at the end of dinner while Don Serapio was hospitably conducting his guest to a sleeping room. Isobel listened to him with interest.

"I've been very stupid," she declared when he finished. "I knew you had a brother who was a soldier. That's how you happened to know Captain Allende. I had forgotten all about him. How do you know he's still with General Calleja?"

"I don't," admitted Nando. "But that's where he was the last time I heard. He may have joined our side by this time."

"It would be only natural that he should." She pulled her long braid over her shoulder and began twisting it between her fingers. "But regardless of which side he's on, I expect you're right. He's almost sure to be in that battle at the Hacienda Marfil."

"Of course he would!" Nando regarded her with admiration. Isobel was really very quick about sorting out bits of information and arriving at conclusions.

"I thought you didn't want to go back to any place where there was fighting," she reminded him shrewdly.

"This is different. Ramón's being there would make it different." Nando put the aftermath of the first battle of Guanajuato firmly from his mind.

"Battles don't last forever, and General Morelos said it was just beginning when he left." She seemed to be thinking aloud as she stood there pulling on her braid. "But if we leave at once, maybe we could make it before it's over."

"We?" cried Nando, his voice rising in protest. "You can't go."

"There'll be lots of creole officers around this time. And I've already told you I was willing to sacrifice my hair."

"But Doña Triumfa would miss you immediately.

She'd send after you, and then we'd both have to come back."

"She'd have to find me first," declared Isobel darkly. But a moment later she gave in. "I know I can't go. But it isn't fair that you should have all the fun and I'm left out of everything just because I was unlucky enough to be born a girl."

"I'll tell you everything when I get back," promised Nando. "Every little thing. Didn't I tell you before?"

"Parts of it I had to drag out of you," remembered Isobel crossly. "Well, go change your clothes. You'd better wear those peon things that Father Hidalgo gave you. I'll go and see about a horse. But mind you don't lose him as you did the burro."

The horse which Isobel led to the door was a sorrel mare. She had long legs, Nando noted with satisfaction, and an inquisitive look in the brown eyes which she turned to him as he stepped forward to take the lines from the girl's hands.

"This is not one of your father's horses," he decided. "At least I've never seen her before."

"Oh, she's not Papa's." Isobel seemed glad that she was no longer responsible for holding the animal. "She belongs to the Conde de la Canal. I just borrowed her."

"But won't the *conde* mind?" gasped Nando. He was very sure that the word "borrowed" would translate into "stole," and he didn't want to be arrested for horse stealing.

"He'll never miss her," declared Isobel positively. "He has lots of horses. Most of them he keeps at his country place. There are only a few stabled here in town, and he hardly ever takes them out."

"But what if he decides to? What if he asks for this particular mare before I get her back?" Even through his protests Nando was busy shortening the long stirrups to his own needs.

"I'll worry about that if it happens," declared Isobel. "I asked the stable boy which was the fastest horse. He told me this one, so I gave him a *peseta* to saddle her for me and another *peseta* to come and warn me if the *conde* should send asking for her. But the boy doesn't think that's likely. La Golondrina is a very small horse, and the *conde* is a large man. He likes to ride bigger horses."

"I'd still feel better if the horse belonged to your father," grumbled Nando. He put a foot in the stirrup and swung to the saddle.

"Papa has only carriage horses," Isobel reminded him, frowning. "He gave up riding years ago. I thought you wanted a fast horse."

"I do," Nando assured her quickly. He turned the mare in the street. Although she had objected to being led, she responded immediately to the signals of a rider. "I'll get back as soon as I can. And thank you, Isobel."

"Just see that you don't lose the *conde*'s horse." she called after him. "And be sure to remember every little thing you see."

La Golondrina lived up to her reputation of being a fast horse. Once they had left the cobblestones of San Miguel el Grande behind, her hooves fairly flew over the dusty road to Dolores.

It was the first time Nando had been on horseback since the day the bandit had pulled him from El Sable. He was filled with a sense of importance whenever they passed a field where peons were working. They always stopped whatever they were doing, staring after him with gaping mouths. The boy realized it was because of the billowing white shirt which marked him as an Indian like themselves.

His training on the hacienda had taught him the proper care of horses, so despite the need for haste he did not push the mare beyond her endurance. He urged her to change her gait often, stopping occasionally for rest and water. La Golondrina seemed to sense what was needed of her, and the long sorrel legs repaid his care.

It was night by the time they reached the mountains, but Nando did not stop. Sometimes the road was too dark for him to see, but the mare picked her way carefully through the black places. When they emerged into open starlight he could see that they were still on course.

Soon after daylight he recognized a familiar landmark off the road. It was the Hacienda de Burras, where Nando had stopped before and fallen in with El Pipila. He turned the mare from the highway into the narrow, winding road which led between barren fields to the white buildings. La Golondrina's head was sagging now, and she raised her long legs slowly. She had earned a rest.

The household servants saw him coming, and they were all huddled in a little group to watch the arrival of the stranger on a horse.

Nando lifted his sombrero high so that they might see his face, and when he replaced it on his head he made sure it was at the careful tilt to show his honesty.

"Why, it's Nando!" Teresa recognized him. He heard her shrill voice calling, and the next moment she pushed forward from the others. "It's the boy who brought us news of the valor of my cousin, El Pipila! Nando, what are you doing here?"

"And why are you on a horse?" called another voice, sharp with censure. "Have you stolen it?"

"No, no. It was loaned to me by one of the Great Ones. And the same Great One sent me to bring back news of the battle." There was no need to explain to these curious peons that the Great One in question was a twelve-year-old girl and that she had stolen the animal.

"The battle," they repeated, and their voices grew awed. Apparently Nando's explanation was accepted, for no one questioned further his right to ride a horse.

"It must have been a terrible thing," declared an old man. "We could hear the voices of the cannon here on the hacienda yesterday. And the place where it was being fought, the Hacienda Marfil, is several miles away."

"Is it over?" demanded Nando quickly. He jumped to the ground and stood beside La Golondrina's drooping head.

"We do not know. We have not heard the guns since yesterday. But we will know when our *patrón* returns. He went to Guanajuato a week ago to visit friends. Soon he should return, and he will bring the news."

"I must go on now. Today," insisted Nando. "The Great One who sent me desires me to return with news as soon as possible. May I leave my horse here to rest, and will you loan me another to continue the trip?"

"We could not loan you a horse!" cried Teresa in a scandalized tone.

"No," agreed the old man, who seemed to be the spokesman for the others. "I do not know the Great One of whom you speak, he who defies the king's orders in permitting you to ride a horse. But we cannot do so."

"Who is this Great One who takes such authority upon himself just to satisfy his own thirst for news? Where does he live?" demanded another voice.

"In San Miguel el Grande. And if he can trust me, why can't you?"

"We have no horses to loan you," explained the old man patiently. "The horses belong to the *patrón*, and as we have told you, he is not here."

"You have mules," Nando reminded him. "If I leave my horse here as security, will you loan me one of them until I return?"

Two or three of the men began whispering together. They were all old, Nando observed. The young men must be away with the army. Finally the little group reached a decision.

"We will loan you a mule," said the spokesman. "It belongs to the uncle of El Pipila, he who behaved with such valor in the battle of Guanajuato. He will loan you his mule if you will attempt to gain news of his nephew, for certainly whatever El Pipila does in this second battle must surpass what he did in the first."

"I will try to find out if I can," promised Nando thankfully.

One of the peons led La Golondrina away, after promising to give her food and water, and returned in a few minutes with a mule.

"This one is not used to a saddle," he explained. "I tried to put on the one which was worn by the Great One's horse, but the stubborn mule would have none of it."

"No matter." Nando reached up to grasp the animal's straggling mane, and the next minute he was on the mule's back.

"Go with God," they shouted, as he kicked the surprised animal ahead. And "We will pray to the Virgin to look after you."

"If you do not return with the mule, the horse

of the Great One is mine to sell," called the *mestizo* uncle of El Pipila.

The Hacienda Marfil was the next estate. Its buildings were concealed from the road, but Nando was unpleasantly aware of its proximity by the number of vultures circling overhead. It was an ominous sight, and he was certain that whatever was concealed beyond the hill would be even more so. But he had to see; he had to make sure.

He had pulled the mule to a halt and was preparing to turn the animal off the road when a small group of men appeared over the crest. They were all peons, and they were progressing very slowly at a pace which was more of a stagger than a walk. Nando's bare heels kicked at the mule to start it ahead, for he could see that some of the men were supporting others, and that all of them were wounded.

"Water!" He could see their lips moving even before he was in earshot, and the word continued as a dismal croak after he had reached them.

"I haven't any," confessed Nando, his eyes staring down at the blood-soaked bandages which they had torn from pieces of shirts. "But I'll get it. I'll get help from the next hacienda. Don't try to walk. Just sit down and wait."

They took him at his word. Without protest, they sank to the ground where they stood.

"Are there any more who live?" asked Nando.

"Any left who were too weak to crawl away from the battlefield?"

"None who live," answered one who seemed a little stronger than the others. "But thousands who are dead. Thousands of the *generalissimo's* men, and a few of the viceroy's, too."

"Where is the rest of the army? The living?"

"Allende led a decoy troop north, and Calleja's men followed. The others marched south under the *generalissimo*," the man told him weakly. "I think they got away."

Nando did not wait to hear more. He rode the mule back over the way he had just traveled. The peons at the Hacienda de Burras would come for the survivors as soon as they knew. And as a Christian, it was Nando's duty to delay his own journey until he had spread the news.

El Pipila's uncle wanted to reclaim his mule as soon as he heard that the greater portion of the army had slipped away. He refused to believe that anyone so daring as his nephew had fallen in battle. Nando hoped he was right. He hated to think that the mighty-shouldered El Pipila was one of the thousands who littered the field at the Hacienda Marfil. But he refused to relinquish the mule, and in the hubbub of arranging burros and litters to carry the wounded, he slipped away.

He had decided that there was nothing for him to do but go on north toward Guanajuato. If Ramón was still with General Calleja, he would be there.

And even if he weren't, Nando was filled with an overwhelming fear for Don Ignacio. A decoy company sounded dangerous! He wanted to make sure that his friend was safe.

When he reached the place where he and El Pipila had first observed the city, Nando stopped and tied the mule behind a thicket off the road. He had already lost one animal in this town. If the same thing happened to the mule, he would not be able to return the *conde*'s horse, and both he and Isobel would be in serious trouble.

From the hillside he could see great activity around the fortress which was the *Alhondiga de Granaditas,* although from this distance he could not make out what all the people were doing there. He could not even tell whether they were civilians or soldiers, although they were there in great numbers. It would be easy enough to lose himself in such a vast crowd, he decided, and by keeping his ears open he might be able to discover the fate of the decoy company.

As he traveled the narrow, sloping streets, Nando thought how strange it was they all were empty. Some of the doors in the walls gaped open, and when he peered inside at the flowered patios, they were empty, too. Whatever was going on at the *Alhondiga* must be important indeed to call everyone away from home.

As soon as he neared his destination, he could see that the outer crowd was made up of soldiers, royalist troops. Unlike the fighting men of Father Hidalgo, even the ordinary soldier in the viceroy's army wore a uniform. Nando was suddenly conscious that his were the only clothes of the lower class on the street.

This was no place for him, he decided. He could not mingle unnoticed among all these warriors. He had just turned to retrace his steps when one of the soldiers spied him.

"Ho! There is one we missed," he shouted gleefully.

Instinctively, Nando started to run. But he was too late, for the next moment he was overtaken. Burly arms fastened themselves about him, holding him fast. The smell of garlic and chili filled his nose as the soldier thrust his face close.

"Come, come, little one, little miner from Guanajuato. Did you think you could hide? General Calleja would not like it if we let you get away. He says we are to put to death every rebel of Guanajuato. And you are no exception."

Nando struggled wildly, but the soldier was stronger. He forced the boy along, sometimes dragging him by the heels, and the crowds opened to let them through. Nando had only glimpses of laughing, jeering faces under military caps as he was pulled along.

"Stop!" he cried frantically. "I am not from Guanajuato. I am not a miner. Stop! You are making a mistake."

"No mistake," laughed the soldier. "Why is it you miners give up your lives with such reluctance?"

"Captain de Fuentes!" cried Nando desperately. "Captain Ramón de Fuentes. Take me to him. Send a message. I must see Captain de Fuentes."

"You must see the firing squad. That is who you must see," said the soldier, hurrying him forward. "Patience now. It will not be long."

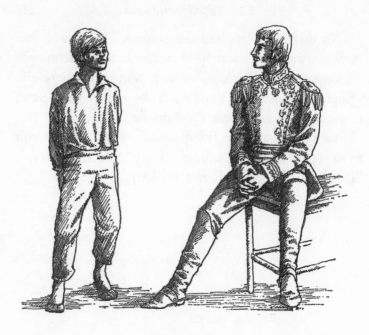

16

The soldier dragged Nando, kicking and screaming his brother's name, through the jeering crowd. No one heeded, rather his outcries seemed to add to their enjoyment of the spectacle. Perhaps, thought Nando wildly, it was the wrong thing to say. Perhaps Ramón had gone over to the liberating army, and the soldiers were the more intent on his own death as a revenge. Well, if that was the case, he'd throw it in their teeth. Raising his head above the knotted arm about his chest, he shrieked with all the lung power at his command.

"Captain de Fuentes! Captain Ramón de Fuentes!"

As they were about to enter the doorway of the *Alhondiga,* a man stepped forward. He was a *mestizo,* wearing the insignia of a noncommissioned officer.

"One moment, soldier. I would have a word with your prisoner."

The soldier who had been dragging Nando stopped, but he did not release his grip. The sergeant regarded Nando carefully.

"Your name?"

"Fernando." The Christian name was enough. They would never have believed a dirty, dark-skinned boy wearing the clothes of a peon had he claimed relationship with a creole officer.

"Where are you from?"

"From the Hacienda del Fuentes. It is north of Puebla, in the mountains." Nando didn't know why he answered in this manner. It would be more believable to say he was from San Miguel el Grande, which was not so far away.

"You are not from Guanajuato?"

"No." Nando shook his head violently. Then he added, "What is happening here? Why have I been taken this way and threatened with execution when I have done nothing to deserve it?"

"You ask too many questions," complained the soldier who was holding him. He turned to the sergeant. "You heard the general's orders. All who are suspected of aiding the rebels in the early battle of Guanajuato are to be executed."

"But this boy says he is not from here," pointed out the sergeant. "He claims to bring a message for my captain, Captain Ramón de Fuentes. A message from his own hacienda."

"They will say anything to save their own lives," sneered the soldier. "What message could have such importance as to send a hacienda-peon pursuing the great captain to the very field of battle?"

The sergeant shrugged. There was something to what the soldier said.

"His father is dead," cried Nando quickly. "That is the message I am to convey to Captain de Fuentes. His father Don Anselmo, *patrón* of the Hacienda del Fuentes, is no longer among the living."

The soldier loosened his grip slightly.

"It has a ring of truth," he admitted with reluctance. "But when I saw him standing there in the streets— And after he started to run—"

"Come with me," ordered the sergeant. "I will take you to my captain. If you are from his hacienda he will know you. And after you have delivered your message, there may be other news of more cheerful nature that you can give him."

As they prepared to leave, a volley of shots rang out from within the *Alhondiga*. The soldier grinned, but the noise went unnoticed by the *mestizo*. He turned and started through the crowd, keeping the fingers of one hand closed about the boy's arm.

The Plaza Mayor was crowded with soldiers, as were all the side streets leading to the *Alhondiga*, but above the heads of the throng Nando glimpsed a structure which made him shiver. It was obviously intended as a gallows, for a row of ropes, each ending with an open noose, dangled from the top beam. He tugged at the sergeant's arm.

"For whom are those intended?" he gasped.

"The town dignitaries," answered the *mestizo*. His tone was noncommittal. "They are to hang there as a warning to any who, in the future, might think it wise to help the rebels."

Nando looked straight ahead. He was glad they had passed by before the execution had taken place.

The sergeant led him to one of the large houses on a street off the square.

"My captain is quartered in this one," he said proudly. "Each of our officers has taken over a house, but to me this is one of the finest. Observe the exquisite carving above the door."

"It was kind of their owners to loan their houses to your officers," said Nando politely.

The *mestizo* smiled without humor.

"Their former creole owners will never need their houses again," he said dryly.

A soldier on duty at the door told them that Captain de Fuentes was in the patio.

"I think he suffers from the indigestion," he confided. "He does not wish to witness the excitement at the *Alhondiga*. And he refused his dinner."

The sergeant nodded, and motioned Nando to follow him. At a doorway leading to the inner garden, he stopped and came to smart attention.

"Captain."

The man sitting in the shade of a spraying fountain glanced up. He wore the blue and white colors of the viceroy, and his feet in polished Spanish boots were stretched out on a second chair. Nando caught his breath. It was all he could do to keep from running across the tiled floor and throwing himself upon his brother. But that would never do. Like an actor in a play, he must stay with the assigned part he was playing.

"I found this boy on the square, Captain. He was calling out your name as they rushed him to the *Alhondiga*," explained the sergeant. For the first time he dropped his matter-of-fact way of speaking. Now his voice grew deeper, filled with expression. It was quite evident that Captain de Fuentes had both his admiration and respect.

"My name?" Ramón lowered his boots to the floor and peered around the fountain at the smaller figure in white cotton which stood behind his sergeant.

"He says he brings you a message from your hacienda. Bad news, my Captain, if he speaks the truth."

"Come here, boy," ordered Ramón.

Nando took the sombrero from his head and started forward. He walked slowly, hoping that Ramón's shock at seeing him would not give them both away.

Ramón's pupils dilated slightly as he stared at the dirty brown face above the white shirt, but he gave no other sign of surprise.

"I know this boy," he said steadily. "He is indeed from my hacienda. I have watched him grow through the years. You did well to save him, Carlos. Thank you."

"For nothing, my Captain. Shall I leave him with you?"

"Yes," agreed Ramón. "Leave him. And tell them to send food. Boys are always hungry, and this one has the look of having traveled far."

As soon as the sergeant had disappeared, Ramón grasped his brother tightly.

"Nando. What are you doing here? And dressed in those clothes?"

"I came looking for you." To his embarrassment, Nando felt his eyes swim with tears. He brushed them away quickly. "And they almost shot me. Ramón, they're killing everyone in Guanajuato. Didn't you know? Why don't you stop them?"

"A captain does not countermand the orders of his general, Nando. If I tried to do that, I'd be as bad as any rebel." Ramón's voice was gruff.

"The rebels aren't bad," corrected Nando. "They're only trying to help Mexico. To help us. I knew you didn't understand, Ramón. That's why I came to find you, to explain it to you."

"Explain what to me?" Ramón stared at him in amazement. Then he smiled. "I don't want to hear politics from you, little brother. I want to hear how you got here, why you're dressed in those clothes, and why you aren't home on the hacienda where you belong."

So Nando sat in one of the chairs and told the whole story of his adventures. Ramón was deeply moved by the news of his father's death. Calleja's troops had been constantly on the march, and the messenger had never reached him. His face grew very stern when he listened to the account of Alejandro's plan to enroll their brother in the priesthood, and even after Nando explained about the letter which told of Alejandro's change of heart the hardness remained. But when the boy went on to relate the other adventures which had befallen him, Ramón kept shaking his head as though the whole thing was beyond his belief.

"Surely the Virgin has taken you in her charge," he decided when Nando had finished. "I have never known anyone to get himself into so many difficulties. If it were not for Our Lady snatching you back each time, you would never have lived through it all."

"But I have," Nando reminded him quickly. "And now that I've found you, I think we should get out of here and go looking for Don Ignacio. I'm worried about him."

"No need. Ignacio can take care of himself." Again Ramón shook his head, this time a little ruefully. "I didn't know it was he who was leading us that chase through the hills, but he made very sure that we lost him. That's when the general decided to march on to Guanajuato and administer punishment to the sympathizers."

"You didn't know that Don Ignacio was one of the leaders? That he is now captain general?"

"Oh yes. I'd heard of that." Ramón frowned. "It's hard to believe that a man whom you have known so many years, a friend with whom you have shared so much, could change as he did. To think that Ignacio could forget his oath, his loyalty to his king and sovereign—"

"But we don't even know who the king of Spain is," interrupted Nando.

Ramón smiled indulgently.

"Those matters will be taken care of by people who are far smarter than we, little brother. We need not concern ourselves. The important thing at the moment is to see that you get back home. I will send Carlos with you, the one who saved you at the *Alhondiga*. Carlos is to be trusted."

"I don't want to go with Carlos," objected Nando. "I want you to come with me, Ramón."

"I can't leave now. We are in the midst of a war, although I don't think it will last much longer. The untrained peons who follow that fanatical priest Hidalgo and my poor misled friend Ignacio are no match for us."

"Father Hidalgo isn't a fanatic," objected Nando hotly. "And Don Ignacio isn't misled. If you knew them better, if you could only hear their side, you wouldn't think so."

"You forget that I've known Ignacio for years," Ramón reminded him dryly. "Of course that was before he was influenced by a heretic."

"Father Hidalgo isn't a heretic!" Nando stood back, his eyes narrowed in anger. "He's a good Christian, as good as you or I. Better, because he reads books which explain many mysteries which we do not understand."

"I have heard that he reads foreign books. Many of them forbidden," said Ramón. "It is right for you to defend him, Nando—up to a point. He was kind to you, and for that reason I, too, am in his debt. But your defense must not be carried too far. The *Inquisición* has judged Father Hidalgo a heretic. Perhaps he is ruled by the devil, and it is the devil who gives him power to sway other men like my poor befuddled friend Ignacio."

"That's not so," denied Nando hotly. "Father Hidalgo is good. And the cause for which he fights is right. If you could only meet him, Ramón, you'd see for yourself."

"I am likely to meet him, but there will be no time for conversation when I do."

"You mean—in battle?" Nando stared at him in disbelief. "Would you—you wouldn't kill him?"

"I would prefer to take him prisoner," Ramón told him. "But you must remember that I am a soldier, Nando. I have my duty to perform."

"And would you kill Don Ignacio, too? Would you kill him in battle?"

"That would be harder for me to do," Ramón answered honestly. "Ignacio was my friend. He is still my friend, for our ties are very deep. But if I had to—if it could not be avoided—"

"You—murderer!" Nando stared at his brother in horror. "That's what you confess to being, a murderer. Oh, I wish I had never come here. I wish I had never seen you. And I never will again! From this day I will not have you for a brother!"

He turned and rushed from the room, down the corridor, past the sentry at the door, and out into the street. He did not know that Ramón followed, calling loudly for Carlos.

"Follow the boy," he ordered the sergeant who answered the summons promptly. "Try not to let him see you if you can, but make sure he is not picked up by any patrol. I think he will take the road to San Miguel el Grande. Return when you see him safely out of Guanajuato, but not before."

17

Three days later Nando rode La Golondrina down the cobblestoned streets of San Miguel el Grande. It was the hour of sunset, and the western sky was slashed with gold across a changing curtain of rose and pink. The plaza was thronged with people who had come from their houses to gather under the lacy trees and gossip with their neighbors.

Nando rode past them without glancing in their direction. The brim of his sombrero was straight above his eyes, for in the great shame which enveloped him how could he wear it otherwise? He had repudiated Ramón, but words could not erase the ties of blood. He was the brother of an affirmed murderer, one who would kill the saintly Father Hidalgo, even his friend Don Ignacio, if he could. The relationship marked Nando with a stain more hideous than the Indian blood of his great-grandmother.

He wanted to atone for that stain with penance, and that was why he rode the stolen mare in front of all the people. They would recognize it, realize what he had done, and punish him accordingly. The payment for one crime, if it was bad enough, might serve to equal out the other.

To his amazement, his appearance was greeted with cheers, which increased in intensity as the crowd recognized the rider. Their *olés* filled the crisp air and set the roosting grackles in the trees to chattering with alarm.

"Nando! Don Fernando!" shouted the people. "Stop! Give us the news!"

Someone dashed from the crowd to grasp the leather bridle, and La Golondrina came to a halt. People stopped walking on the winding paths, they jumped up from the ornate iron benches, and now they jammed the streets so that further progress was impossible.

"The news," they kept repeating. "Give us the battle news which you brought from the Hacienda Marfil!"

"It was a bloody battle," reported Nando obediently. "General Calleja won. Thousands of our brave men perished, but the losses of our enemy were very small."

The crowd moaned in disappointment.

"Go on. Go on," prompted a sharp voice with so much authority that Nando continued.

"Father Hidalgo—the *generalissimo*—escaped with the main portion of the army. They went south. And the Captain General Allende led a decoy company north, which Calleja's men followed. He eluded them in the mountains and escaped."

At this the people cheered loudly and with especial pride. Don Ignacio was one of theirs. Had he not been born in San Miguel el Grande?

"Go on," ordered the same authoritative voice as before. This time it came from just below. Nando stared down into the thin, aristocratic face of the Conde de la Canal.

"I stole your horse, señor," he admitted bravely. "I, and no other, am responsible. You may punish me as you see fit."

"The only punishment will be for withholding information," replied the *conde*. "I am honored that my mare had a small part in bringing news so quickly to our town. Although," he added dryly, "the Señorita Isobel Rodriguez may dispute your claims as being solely responsible. She has already confessed her role in the little plot which you two conceived to keep us informed."

Nando's mouth dropped open. That Isobel! Who

else would think to explain the sin of theft as an act of public service?

"Surely you discovered something else?" insisted the *conde* anxiously.

Nando nodded weakly.

"After he lost the trail of the captain general, Calleja went on to Guanajuato. There he executed everyone who might be sympathetic to our cause. The peons were shot in the *Alhondiga*. The creoles were hanged in the square. He said it was a lesson to anyone who might think to take sides against the viceroy."

There was a long moment of hushed silence. Then people began to cry out in protest. This was a deed so low that they could hardly find words to express their feelings against its perpetrators. Instead of resulting in obedience to the king's laws, it was having an opposite effect. Those who had hesitated on the borderline now swung over to the side of freedom.

"Get down, my boy. Get down."

Don Serapio had finally squeezed his fat little person through the crowd. He stood beside the *conde*, beaming with pride as he looked up at the rider.

"You have had a hard journey. Everyone knows it. You have been through a most difficult and dangerous experience. You must come home now and enjoy the rest which you have so amply earned."

People were pressed so closely that it was all

Nando could do to slide down from the saddle. The *conde* called one of his servants to lead La Golondrina back to her stable, and Nando followed the *alcalde* through the path made by the admiring crowd.

Only once did Don Serapio reprove Nando for what he had done. That was as they paused, waiting for the servant to open the door below the carved cherubs.

"If you had told me your plans beforehand, I would have stopped you. It was very dangerous, and required a great deal of courage. Yes, I should certainly have stopped you from going had I known." Then he added, as though speaking to himself, "In which case it would have been days, perhaps weeks, before we would have found out the news."

Isobel was proud of his exploits, too, but she was equally proud of the way she had explained the *conde*'s mare.

"The silly man decided to take her out for a canter the very next day after you left," she told Nando. "And that good-for-nothing stable boy said I had come and taken her—after I'd given him two *pesetas*, too. The *conde* came to Papa, of course, and they both sent for me, so there was nothing to do but admit it. I told them that I had borrowed the mare so that you could ride quickly to the Hacienda Marfil."

"That part was the truth," agreed Nando, who

still couldn't understand why everyone insisted on making a hero of him.

"Of course," Isobel smiled widely. "They caught me by surprise. I didn't have a chance to think of anything else. But when the *conde* said, 'Merciful Mother, no news is worth risking the life of a creole. Why didn't they send an *Indito*?' Why then it came to me."

"What?"

"Why, I reminded them that a peon couldn't ride a horse. It had to be a creole, who knew how to handle one properly, as you do. And I told them that since you were too young to fight, this was your way of doing something for your fellow countrymen. You wanted to show your patriotism by bringing back a firsthand account of what was going on."

Nando shook his head silently. He still couldn't understand how things had turned out as they had.

"I didn't tell them it was because you really wanted to see your brother," concluded Isobel. "Did you find him?"

Nando drew himself up haughtily. "I have no brother," he said coldly. "Except Alejandro. The brother Ramón, whom I used to have, is no more." There was something in his expression which prevented even Isobel from questioning him further.

Once again the people of San Miguel el Grande were forced to depend upon the reports of their paid messengers. But for a time, at least, the news continued every few weeks.

Hidalgo had fled with his army to Guadalajara, and when he arrived, he found the city open to him. Previous to his arrival, the residents of that city had organized their own army and had already imprisoned the *gachupines* and those with royalist leanings.

The *generalissimo* took advantage of the public printing press and sent manifestos throughout the land, putting forth his policies. He did not seek to change the form of government, he said in bold black type, but only to free Mexico from the Spanish yoke and to make the rule less absolute. Also he denied all charges made against him of heresy.

Don Serapio had a copy of the manifesto, and almost wore it out from handling it so often.

"If he reads it to me one more time, I'll scream," declared Isobel bitterly. "I already know the whole thing by heart from having to listen to it so often."

"But it gives him so much pleasure to read it to us," explained Nando.

He had grown very quiet since his return from Guanajuato. Everyone said it was modesty, and most becoming in a hero. But it was really because Nando could not keep his thoughts away from Ramón.

Perhaps he himself had been at fault in rushing away. Perhaps he should have stayed and tried to make Ramón understand about Father Hidalgo, and the true reasons behind the rebellion. But Ramón wouldn't have listened. He was one of the viceroy's men, and an enemy to Mexico.

But he wasn't an enemy of Nando. No matter what Ramón did, Nando would always love his brother. The momentary hatred had burned itself out. Some of the shame remained, and a great fear for what Ramón, as a soldier, might do. But the shame no longer included Nando himself. He was his own man, a separate entity. And he was on the side of justice and freedom.

Christmas week brought something to think about besides Ramón and loyalties. It was the first Christmas Nando had ever spent away from the hacienda, and it was different being in a town with many people. Strangers thronged the streets, instead of the familiar peons he had known all his life. The *parroquia* was larger and grander here. The *posada*, in which he took part, visited great houses, not Indian huts, and ended at the fine mansion of the Conde de la Canal, where Nando's was the lucky stick to break the *piñata*. He was glad there was nothing to remind him of home, for he wouldn't want anyone to know how much he missed it.

He dreaded most of all the day of the Three Kings, for this year he had no money to buy gifts for anyone. Don Serapio must have sensed his humiliation, for two days before he pressed some coins into the boy's hand.

"An early present," he whispered, smiling. "Use it as you will."

So Nando bought gifts after all, a lace-embroidered handkerchief for Doña Triumfa, a silver pin for Don Serapio, a string of small opal beads for Isobel, and from the market, small remembrances for the servants. He would have liked to buy presents for Don Ignacio and Father Hidalgo, who had been so kind to him, but they were not here, and no one could tell when the war would be at an end so they could return.

One day when they were alone, he found courage to ask Don Serapio about this. The little *alcalde's* pink face grew very solemn.

"I do not know, Nando," he admitted. "No one knows. But," his voice sank to a whisper, "can you keep a secret?"

Nando nodded silently. He couldn't imagine why Don Serapio was telling him something which he wouldn't even divulge to his own daughter.

"If all else fails, if we find ourselves facing nothing but reverses, we shall seek outside aid," he confided. "In the United States, which is a great country north of here, there is a group of men who once promised to come to our assistance if we ever struck for liberty. You see, only a few years ago, the United States was in a position not unlike the one in which we find ourselves. Only at that time they belonged to England, not to Spain. The leader of this sympathetic group is a military man.

He helped to win their war, and he has promised to help us. His name is Colonel Aaron Burr."

"Oh," whispered Nando. It made him feel very important to be entrusted with such an important secret. He hoped that Isobel would never guess that he knew something she didn't.

After Christmas, the messengers began coming once more to San Miguel el Grande. Calleja had attacked Guadalajara. Again he had put the liberating forces to route. He had exploded an ammunition wagon in their faces, the flames had caught the dried grasses of the battlefield, and the wind had blown it into the advancing forces of Hidalgo's men. Thousands were killed, and other thousands had deserted. Some of them began drifting back to take up their former work in San Miguel el Grande.

The sight of one of these returned soldiers never failed to throw Don Serapio into a fury. Wherever he was, he stopped to deliver a lecture to the unhappy peon, and people could hear him for blocks around.

It was spring now, and Holy Week was upon them. Children cracked raw eggs on the heads of the unwary who chanced to occupy one of the iron benches of the plaza. Already the days were growing uncomfortably warm, and the air did not even cool by night.

A messenger came again, and was closeted for some time with the *alcalde*. When he finally left the meeting, tears were running down Don Serapio's pink cheeks, and he would not stop in answer to Doña Triumfa's anxious call, but trotted straight out of the door.

"Come on, Nando," ordered Isobel, jumping up and starting after her father.

"Isobel," protested Doña Triumfa. "It is not seemly! Come back!"

But Isobel would not come back, and with a murmured apology Nando hurried after her. In a moment Doña Triumfa herself arose and went to apply a curious eye to a crack in the front door.

Don Serapio went straight to the *parroquia*. He was inside for only a few moments before the great bell in the tower began to ring. It was not the steady clang, clang, clang which summoned the worshipers to mass. The wielder of the rope had been impressed by the importance of Don Serapio's mission, and now his body was plainly visible in the tower, swinging up and down as fast as he could place his feet upon the floor.

At first the other church bells were silent, but there was an affinity among the bell ringers of San Miguel el Grande. They often played games, seeing who could outdrown the other with the iron voice of his charge. Perhaps they sensed the urgency in the tempo of the *parroquia's* bell, for now they all began to ring at once, and the mighty pealing echoed against the surrounding hills.

Immediately people began gathering upon the plaza before the largest church. Work was left unfinished, sleepers awoke from naps, the young and old, beggars and aristocratic creoles crowded the square and stood looking up at the *parroquia* steps where the *Alcalde* Rodriguez waited alone and wept unashamed.

Finally, when it seemed that the square could hold no more, when certainly everyone within hearing who had legs to walk upon was gathered there, Don Serapio looked up and signaled to the bell ringer. The iron voice of the *parroquia* was still, and one by one the other ringers dropped their ropes and hurried down from their towers so that they, too, might hear the message.

"I have sad news," began the *alcalde* bravely. "Prepare yourselves. The *generalissimo,* our own Father Hidalgo from the neighboring village of Dolores, is taken prisoner."

Instantly there was a great moaning from the people gathered in the plaza. They fell down on their knees, and the sound of a thousand prayers filled the air.

Father Hidalgo taken, thought Nando. A prisoner! Across his mind flashed the memory of that pile of fagots before the cathedral in Mexico City. Those had been for a heretic, and heresy was the accusation placed at Hidalgo's door.

"We have not received many particulars," continued the *alcalde* in a choked voice, and the prayers halted so that people could hear every word. "He was on his way to the United States to ask for their aid in our fight for freedom. With him were Captain General Allende, Juan Aldama—who is known to all of you in San Miguel—and two other officers whose names I do not know. They fell into an ambuscade at a place called Acatita de Baján. They were put in chains and are being forced to march to Chihuahua, there to stand trial."

"I know that country," called an angry voice. "It is barren, hard. And it is six hundred miles from Acatita to Chihuahua. Too far for the crippled leg of an old man like Father Hidalgo to walk."

"I have told you all I know," admitted Don Serapio miserably. "Let us pray to the Virgin. Only she can help us now."

Although the leaders had been taken late in March it was almost June before word of their capture reached San Miguel el Grande. After that, weeks went by before they heard anything else. Every day the churches were crowded, and the supplicants repeated a single prayer: save Father Hidalgo, Don Ignacio, and Juan Aldama. For Aldama's brother, the *Licenciado* Ignacio, there was no hope. He had been taken prisoner by the Spaniards before this, and news of his immediate execution had already been received by the town.

The wonder was that the authorities were delaying the punishment of these others, for the viceroy had long since published an edict that any rebel caught must stand before a firing squad within fifteen minutes after capture. Why did they wait so long this time? Why did they drag the already condemned men in heavy chains across six hundred miles of arid desert? No one knew the answer, but while there was known life the people continued to pray.

The summer was unusually wet that year. Perhaps the skies, too, wept for the cause of freedom which seemed lost. The people of San Miguel el Grande went about their daily chores as they had always done, everyone saving what he could for the taxes, which would now be even heavier than before.

For some weeks, Nando had been making plans of his own. There was no one he could send with a letter to Alejandro, and no one here he could ask for money to finance his trip home. But it was time for him to go, and there was only one way to get there. He would have to travel on his two feet. Dressed in the clothes of a peon, he would be safe from bandits, and he knew now that he was not too proud to beg food along the way.

He had waited until the rainy season was at an end, and now he was determined to announce his plans to the Rodriguez family following dinner. But something Doña Triumfa said made him say the words a little earlier.

"Fernando needs new clothes, Don Serapio," she declared, putting down her fork and regarding Nando critically. "He has only one suit, and that a little threadbare. Besides, he is growing out of it. Look at his wrists!"

Don Serapio made small clucking noises of distress.

"Someone should have mentioned it before. Tomorrow, Nando, we will go shopping for new clothes for you."

"No," said Nando quickly. By the astonished looks on their faces he realized that he must have sounded rude. There was nothing to do now but explain.

"You see," he said awkwardly, "I'm going to leave. This week. I must go home, to the hacienda. I couldn't wear the new clothes."

"Why not?" asked Doña Triumfa sharply. "Do you wish your brother to think you have been stopping with paupers?"

"It's because of the way I'm going to travel. I'll have to walk. I haven't any money. Alejandro tried to send it, but it didn't arrive."

"You have heard from your brother?" asked the *alcalde* in surprise.

"I had a letter, weeks ago. He wanted me to come home by *diligencia*. And he sent the money. But the messenger didn't leave it. He only left the letter."

"You should have told me at once," declared Don Serapio sternly. "There are ways of dealing with thieves."

"You have to catch one first," Isobel reminded

him. She looked at Nando, and for some unexplained reason she wrinkled her nose in irritation.

"Your poor brother will be worried not to hear from you," chided Doña Triumfa. "You should have told us when the letter first came. Don Serapio would have been glad to advance your fare."

"But he had so many expenses," protested Nando. "He had to pay for all those messengers. And he was very short of money just then."

"Nonsense. I only paid my share for the messengers. The sum was divided among all the creoles here," protested Don Serapio. He looked at Nando curiously. "Who told you I was short of money?"

"I did." Two red spots burned beneath the freckles on Isobel's cheeks. "If I hadn't, he'd have gone away. And it's been pleasant to have him here. He gives me someone to talk to."

"Isobel María Teresa Magdalena Rodriguez!" cried her mother in horrified tones. "You will make confession of that sin before nightfall. Don Serapio, did you ever hear of anything so outrageous as this behavior of your daughter?"

"Never," agreed the *alcalde,* but his eyes twinkled slightly. "Your behavior is most unseemly in a young lady, Isobel. Although I must confess that I, too, have enjoyed the company of Nando."

"We will get a letter off to your brother Don Alejandro at once," promised Doña Triumfa. "But you will not go on foot, dressed like a peon. You will have new clothes, suitable garments for a creole gentleman. And you will go by *diligencia,* providing it is still operating. Is that not so, Don Serapio?"

"Naturally," agreed the *alcalde* quickly.

One of the *criadas* had slipped into the room and now stood hesitating by the door. Doña Triumfa frowned at this interruption of her dinner hour, then beckoned the maid forward.

"It's a gentleman, a soldier, to see Don Serapio," she whispered. "I tried to send him away, but he won't go."

Don Serapio looked up, his pink cheeks quivering with excitement.

"Did he say who he was? What he wanted?"

"No, señor. He said only that he was a friend of Don Ignacio Allende, and that you had something here which belongs to him."

"Show him in. At once," cried Don Serapio. And in explanation to his wife's uplifted eyebrows, "Doubtless he has come from a long way. He will require food."

"Then Don Ignacio's still alive!" cried Isobel, putting into words the thought which had come instantly to every mind. "He wouldn't be sending us a friend if that wasn't so."

No one answered. The room grew silent, as though each one around the table was holding his breath. Through the open doorway leading into the hall, they could hear the metallic clink of spurs striking against the tiled floor.

A moment later the figure of a man filled the

opening. He was tall, with fair hair, and he wore the dusty uniform of an officer in the viceroy's army.

"Don Serapio Rodriguez?" His eyes had gone automatically to the head of the table.

But before Don Serapio could reply, Nando was across the room, clutching the man with both arms about his waist.

"Ramón," he cried in a voice shaking with emotion. "Ramón!"

18

"Ramón!" repeated Isobel, staring across the room. "But you're dead! Nando said so. He said his brother Ramón was no more!"

"As you see, señorita, I am quite alive." Ramón smiled at her briefly.

Don Serapio started from his chair at this announcement. Now he hesitated, his eyes a little troubled as he stared at the blue and white uniform.

"You come from Captain General Allende, señor. You bring us news of him?"

"Dead." Ramón spoke with a soldier's bluntness.

"He was shot, with his face against a wall, and so were Aldama, Jiminez, and Santa Maria."

Doña Triumfa gave a loud cry and buried her face in the lace of her handkerchief.

"And Father Hidalgo?" The *alcalde's* lip trembled, but he forced his voice to continue.

"He, too," replied Ramón. "Although his execution was delayed a month. First he had to be degraded from his priesthood. The bishop came from Durango for that. Then there was the farce of a trial, but in the end it was all the same. He was shot like the others."

Don Serapio teetered backward, groping to find a chair to sit in.

Nando had been so happy only a moment ago, now he was frozen with horror.

"Why didn't you stop it?" He looked up at his brother. "Why did you let them do it?"

"I would have stopped it if I could," said Ramón sadly. "Do you think it is easy to stand by while your best friend is shot as a traitor? But it was Ignacio's wish that I do so. And it was also his wish that I go to his friend, Father Hidalgo, and spend as much time with him as was permitted."

"His wish?" gasped Isobel. "You mean he wanted you to watch him get killed?"

"Don Serapio, I feel your daughter should leave the room. This sordidness is not for tender ears." Doña Triumfa lifted her dripping eyes momentarily from her handkerchief.

"Go away, Isobel," said her father obediently. He continued speaking to his guest. "Please sit down, señor. I am correct in assuming that you are Nando's brother?"

"I am Ramón de Fuentes. And until a month ago I served under the command of General Calleja." His tone was formal. "At that time I left his service, but because of the circumstances of my recent affiliation perhaps you would prefer that I take my brother and quit your house?"

"Please to sit down. You will take something to eat first," suggested the *alcalde* politely.

"Even the enemy can bring news, Don Ramón," observed Isobel sweetly. "And we have had none for months."

"Isobel!" This time it was Don Serapio who was aroused by her impudence. "Leave the room!" He bowed to his guest, "We would be grateful for anything you can tell us, Captain."

"About the deaths of your friends, I can only say that they died bravely, and as gentlemen," replied Ramón stiffly. He did not take one of the chairs at the table, but stood where he was. "I was able to spend some hours with Ignacio before the end. We talked a great deal. At first I could not understand his reasons for taking arms against the viceroy. But I listened. And afterward I explained to him why I had remained in my old command."

"Why had you?" demanded Isobel, leaning forward on her elbows.

Ramón's glance in her direction was a little annoyed.

"When one enters the Army one swears an oath of allegiance, señorita. I took mine seriously. So did Ignacio in those years we spent together. When the Army is your career it becomes like your father. It provides for your welfare, and you, in turn, offer a son's devotion. But Ignacio was sent here, to a town which had always been his home. He saw a different side to life in Mexico, one which was not walled in by barracks. He became close to the people, as a soldier in the field can never do. He saw their needs, their handicaps, the potential which was denied to them."

Doña Triumfa sobbed loudly.

"When did you decide that you'd been wrong and that Don Ignacio was right, Ramón?" Nando looked up at the familiar face, usually so smiling, but today solemn and grave.

"I began to have my doubts in Guanajuato." Ramón mussed his brother's hair. "That wholesale massacre must have taken many innocent bystanders. Why, it almost took you! And then when I saw my friend in chains, for only doing what he thought was right—" His face grew hard. "They did not even take off the chains at night after a hard day's march."

"Was that when you talked to him?" asked Nando. "At night?"

Ramón nodded.

"I would have turned in my commission then," he told them. "Only Ignacio pleaded with me to wait. I would have had to leave immediately, and even then he knew there would be a delay in Father Hidalgo's execution. He wanted someone, a friend, nearby, in case there might be opportunity for escape. But there was none."

"It's too bad you didn't come to this decision before the war was over. We needed officers." Isobel's tone was heavy with censure.

"But the war is not over, señorita." Ramón looked across the table with surprise. "What made you think the war is over?"

"With our leaders dead—" Don Serapio's plump hands waved a gesture of futility.

"Father Hidalgo and Ignacio are dead," agreed Ramón, and Nando felt the hard arm tighten about his shoulders. "But the seeds they have sown have sprouted. I don't suppose you have heard of a priest named Morelos?"

"Why, yes. Yes. He was a guest in this very house. At this very table." Don Serapio's eyes began to glitter with hope. He waved toward the empty chair. "Pray sit down, Captain de Fuentes. Tell us more of the Lieutenant General Morelos and his progress in the south."

"When I return I can tell you better." Ramón still ignored the invitation to sit down. "I am on my way there now. It was the wish of Ignacio and Father Hidalgo that I go to offer my services to

Morelos. His dispatches informed them that in the lands south of Mexico City he has succeeded in raising an army of nine thousand men. His need is for trained officers—"

Don Serapio sprang to his feet, his face radiant. This time he would not take no. He pulled the captain forward, pushing him into the chair and calling loudly for a clean plate.

"Captain, you must forgive us. We were overcome by the suddenness of your arrival. It chased all thoughts of proper courtesy from our heads. But now we have recovered our wits, and you must let us tell you how proud we are that you are here, and how overjoyed we are at the news that the fight for freedom continues."

Even Isobel smiled her appreciation.

"You really had us fooled, Don Ramón. We thought you were the enemy come to gloat. Or come to take Nando away."

Ramón turned to look at his brother, who was hanging over the back of the chair, unwilling to return to his own. For the first time there was that familiar, infectious smile.

"Do you want to go home, Nando?"

"I'd rather go with you," said Nando. "You could teach me to be a brave soldier like you."

"War is not a pretty thing," Ramón shook his head firmly. "Perhaps, when you are older. But not now."

Nando knew that his brother was remembering the massacre at Guanajuato. He did not argue.

"Then I think I'd like to go home," he decided. "Back to the hacienda."

"I've come to take you," agreed Ramón promptly. "We will need men to continue the war. I believe I can enlist many from among our own people and from the adjoining haciendas."

Isobel stood up. Her hands clenched, and under the freckles her face grew very pink. She stared hard at Nando, so overcome with emotion that at first she could not find words.

"You—you burro!" she declared finally, then turned and rushed from the room.

Although the sun had barely cleared the horizon, the peons were at work in the fields when Ramón and Nando rode out of San Miguel el Grande. After the summer rains the land looked fresh and satisfied. An approaching wood-seller returning from the mountains, his burro piled high under a load of mesquite, turned his animal to the side so that the two horsemen would have ample room to pass. He gave the uniformed officer the nodded salute due his rank but stared with disbelief at the other figure, obviously a peon, who dared to ride a horse.

Nando waved merrily, then tilted his sombrero on the back of his head. At least the peon would know him to be an honest man!

Ramón laughed.

"Are you sure it was wise, little brother, to wear

those clothes for the long ride home? Perhaps you should have worn your good suit, or stayed long enough to buy another."

"The clothes Don Ignacio bought me had grown too tight. I would have split the seams. And if we'd waited to have a new one made, it would have meant a longer delay in getting started," explained Nando patiently. He was struck by a fearful thought and looked over at the other rider anxiously. "Unless you are ashamed, Ramón. Unless you feel it is a disgrace to be seen with someone who looks like an *Indito*."

"Don't talk like a fool," said Ramón cheerfully.

"But I do, you know." Nando could not let the subject drop. "I do look like one. At least, I look like the *mestizo* that I am."

Ramón stopped smiling.

"So you know about our illustrious great-grandmother? Then kindly remember that I share her blood the same as you."

"But you don't show it!"

"It is there just the same. And lucky for both of us that it is, or we wouldn't be here. The de Fuentes line would have ended with Great-Grandpapa."

Nando hadn't thought of that before. Perhaps he did owe something to this Indian woman whom he had never seen.

"More than half the creoles I knew in the Army are the same," continued Ramón in a conversational tone. "Only some of their ties are even closer. There is Agustín de Iturbide, for instance. His father was pure Spanish, but his mother is a native of Valladolid, a pure *Indito*."

"And do—is he called a *mestizo?*"

"Captain de Iturbide called a *mestizo?*" Ramón laughed heartily. "No one would dare! He is too brave, too cunning! He would have the skin of anyone who let his tongue slip in such a manner. No, he is a creole gentleman, Nando, as are you."

"But what if one of his grandchildren turns out the way I did? What if he shows only the Indian?"

Ramón grew thoughtful.

"I am a soldier. My thoughts are trained to consider battles," he admitted slowly. "But Ignacio had pondered other matters—"

"So had Father Hidalgo," put in Nando, instantly diverted. "I think they discussed many things together."

"Perhaps the idea came first from the *cura* then," agreed Ramón. "For I admit that it sounded strange on the lips of a creole reared as was our friend. He told me that sometime—not in our lifetime, or even in that of our children—the people of Mexico will be as one. There will be the rich and the poor, for the Bible says they will be always with us. But there will be no thought of mingling of blood strains. We will not be creole or *mestizo*. We will be Mexicans."

"That sounds like Father Hidalgo," decided Nando, smiling. "He was ever the dreamer."

But half the weight was lifted from his shoulders. Ramón shared his burden willingly—and Ramón did not seem to think it even mattered.

Epilogue

Don Fernando Genero Diego Rómolo de Fuentes opened the doorway of his house and stood looking out into the courtyard. It was his thirty-fifth birthday, which luckily fell on his Saint's Day, and as such was celebrated by the workers on his hacienda as a special holiday. He had already attended mass in the small chapel, and was dressed in his new fawn-colored velvet with the opal buttons. Around his waist was a wide blue sash, a gift from his wife, Doña Isobel, who was at this moment in the kitchens overseeing the cooks in their preparations for the feast which would take place later in the day.

Don Fernando did not feel thirty-five today, but he must be for the year was 1832. When he looked back, however, so many changes had been crowded into the time since his father, Don Anselmo, had been the *patrón*, that he could almost believe he was older.

As he stood there looking across the cobblestoned courtyard, some of the old memories rushed up to him. How welcome had been the sight of these white, red-roofed buildings glittering in the sun, the day he and Ramón had ridden in from San Miguel el Grande. San Miguel de Allende, he corrected himself, for the town had changed its name to honor its most revered citizen. And little Dolores had added Hidalgo to its name in memory of the *cura* who was now called "Father of Mexico's Independence."

Don Fernando remembered how, on that day of their arrival, all the peons had stared, especially at his own white dirty garments. It had taken a long time for them to recover from the spectacle of the young son of the household dressed in such a manner. They could not accept him that way. Even when he tilted his sombrero to show his good intentions, they could only stare. So Nando had discarded the loose, white clothes and dressed ever since in a manner more fitting in their eyes.

He remembered the first few days which he and Ramón had spent at home. Only Don Anselmo was sorely missing. They had talked much about their father, he and Ramón, and decided what he would wish them to do.

Nando was to stay at the hacienda and eventually take over as *patrón*. Porfirio, the old foreman, could be trusted to help, for Porfirio had lived there all his life and knew exactly how Don Anselmo wished things done.

Ramón had said that Alejandro would come and visit occasionally, and he was right. Alejandro did visit from time to time, with his wife, Doña Florinda, but they preferred life in Puebla and always returned soon to that city.

As for Ramón, he was a soldier and would never

be anything else. After a few days he left the hacienda with his recruited company of peons and joined Morelos in the south. He was still with the fighting priest two years later at the organization of the national council at Chilpancingo, which declared the Independence of Mexico from Spain and published a constitution.

Then Morelos had been captured and shot, like the saintly Hidalgo, but Ramón had escaped. He continued to fight with the *guerrilla,* and partly due to his influence this group had joined with the creoles and the clergy in supporting de Iturbide in the final overthrow of their mutual enemy. Although de Iturbide's tenure in office was brief, this son of a Spaniard and an Indian girl had done much to erase the stigma of the word *mestizo.* Why, you hardly heard it used any more!

A horseman was approaching across the courtyard, and Don Fernando shaded his eyes, for he had to look into the sun to see.

It was Cardito, who had taken over the job of foreman since the death of his father, Porfirio. Cardito didn't have to remain on the hacienda. He stayed by choice. No longer did a son inherit the debts of his father, and wages had even been raised a few *pesetas.* Life was pleasant on the Hacienda del Fuentes.

"The fireworks have arrived, Don Nando," called Cardito, bringing his horse to a smart stop before the door. As he talked, he leaned down to stroke the animal's sleek neck. "Shall I put Pablo in charge? His is the best hand with fireworks."

"As you will, Cardito." Don Fernando smiled at his old friend. "I leave the arrangements for to-night's entertainment in your capable hands."

Cardito nodded and cantered proudly away.

Through the doorway behind him came his wife, Doña Isobel María Teresa Magdalena. Time had dealt kindly with her. From an impish girl, she had grown into a beautiful woman, with red-brown hair piled high upon her head and a smooth, fair skin on which only the tiniest hint of freckles remained.

"Have you seen our eldest son?" she asked anxiously. "Or his sister? They have been gone since early morning, and I am beginning to worry."

"Miguel can take care of himself, and of Ana, too," Don Fernando turned to assure her smilingly. "He is thirteen, and at that age I traveled on foot all the way from Mexico City to San Miguel."

"You rode on the step of our coach," she corrected.

"Oh, but that was even harder!"

With the speeding grace of the wind which blows through a field of sprouted maize, a boy came racing around the corner of the ranch house. He was fair and slight of build, but seemed unusually tall for his age.

"Father," he cried. "You'll never guess. We've found a herd of bulls quite close to the house. Ana is watching over them until I return."

"A *coleada* of the bulls!" Don Fernando's eyes sparkled. "The very thing to celebrate my Saint's Day, Miguel."

"Not today! At least send Ana back to the house. A girl cannot act the *coleador!*" cried Doña Isobel.

But the two of them had already disappeared around the corner, and she fell silent, shaking her head. Even if he delivered the message, Ana would get around her father somehow. She always did.

Author's Note

September 16 is a national holiday in Mexico. It commemorates the anniversary of that eventful morning when Father Hidalgo gathered six hundred men in front of the *parroquia* in Dolores, and together they marched south to San Miguel. For Father Hidalgo was a real man, and I have tried, as best I could, to give the beginnings of the long revolution which won the Mexican independence.

There are other true characters in the book, Ignacio Allende, the two Aldamas, El Pipila, Doña Josefa and her husband, Don Miguel Dominguez, and the fighting priest José Morelos. If you visit Mexico you will see statues erected in their honor, and towns and streets named after them.

Nando and Isobel, with their respective families, came out of my imagination.

Glossary

Alcalde	Mayor, justice of the peace
Ayuntamiento	Council
Chico	Little boy; *chica*, little girl
Coleada	Game or contest on horseback, which consists of twisting the tail of an unsuspecting bull
Coleador	One who takes part in the *coleada*
Conde	Count, Earl
Conquistadores	The Spaniards who accompanied Cortez in his conquest of Mexico
Corregidor	Magistrate
Creole	A pure-blooded Spaniard born in Mexico
Criada	Maid
Cura	Parish priest
Diligencia	Company of coaches and armed horsemen traveling together for mutual protection
Gachupín	A Spaniard born in Spain
Garbanzo	Vegetable, chick-pea
Hacienda	An estate held by *creoles* or *gachupines;* usually a grant from the king of Spain; many were one hundred square miles in area

Indio; Indito	Indian, native
Inquisición	A tribunal for examination and punishment of heretics
Intendente	Government official
Jicima	A root vegetable
Licenciado	A lawyer
Maguey	Cactus, century plant
Matador	A bullfighter
Mesquite	A species of bush or small tree
Mestizo	One of mixed blood, part Spanish and part Indian
Mirador	Looking-out place on roof of house
Muchacho	Boy
Olé	Bravo, Hurrah!
Parroquia	Parish church; usually used to refer to the largest church in town
Patrón	Owner of hacienda; employer
Peon	Native laborer
Peseta	Small Spanish coin
Piñata	A bowl covered with papier-mâché which holds toys. It is broken by knocking with a stick during parties or in Christmas festivities
Posada	An inn. In the sense used in the book, it is a processional held at Christmas in commemoration of Mary's and Joseph's search for lodgings
Ranchero	Small farmer, rancher
Real	Spanish coin made of silver

Rebozo	Long shawl worn by native women as head covering or wrap
Sala de recibo	Parlor; literally room for receiving guests
Sarape	Woven blanket worn by native men as a cloak
Siesta	Afternoon rest
Sombrero	Wide-brimmed hat
Zócalo	Square or plaza

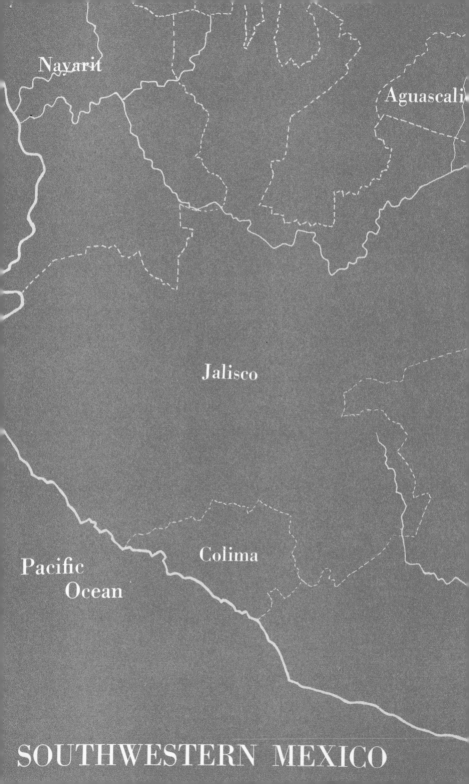